MW01174553

TIME FOR A REAL ADVENTURE

Something caught Stevie's eye over Phil's shoulder. On a sale table near the cash register was a display of trip journals—little red plaid books of blank pages to write on. "Hey!" she cried. "I've got a great idea! Let's each get one of these and keep a diary of our trip. Then, when we get back home, we can share them with each other. It'll be like writing one long letter full of all the interesting stuff we might forget."

"That is a great idea." Phil turned around and grabbed two journals off the shelf. He handed one to her. "One for you and one for me. That way I'll learn all about the Oregon Trail and you'll learn all about white-water rafting. It's almost like going on two vacations."

"Well, almost, but not quite." Stevie laughed. "Look, I've got to go. I hope you have a wonderful trip, Phil."

Phil gave her a gentle smile. "Same here, Stevie. I'll call you as soon as I get back to town." He waved to Lisa and Carole. "Have a great vacation! I'm sure the Oregon Trail will never be the same!"

the Saddle Club

Wagon Trail +
Quarter Horse

Bonnie Bryant

RANDOM HOUSE AUSTRALIA

Random House Australia Pty Ltd
20 Alfred Street, Milsons Point, NSW 2061
http://www.randomhouse.com.au

Sydney   New York   Toronto
London   Auckland   Johannesburg

Random House Australia edition 2003

National Library of Australia
Cataloguing-in-Publication Data

        Bryant, Bonnie.
        Wagon trail + Quarter horse.

        For primary children.
        ISBN 1 74051 841 1.

        1. Horses - Juvenile fiction. 2. Riding clubs - Juvenile
        fiction. I. Bryant, Bonnie. Quarter horse. II. Title.
        III. Title : Wagon trail and Quarter horse. (Series :
        Bryant, Bonnie. Saddle Club).

        813.54

*I would like to express my special thanks
to Sallie Bissell for her help
in the writing of this book.*

*Thanks also to Ellen Levine,
who helped me find the trail.*
—B.B.

"WHEW!" STEVIE LAKE unbuckled her riding helmet and wiped the sweat from her forehead. "I don't think I've ever gone over so many cavalletti in one hour. I was beginning to feel like a Mexican jumping bean."

Carole Hanson smiled as she clipped her horse, Starlight, to a set of cross-ties. "I know what you mean, Stevie. But just think. If you feel like a Mexican jumping bean, then these horses must feel like kangaroos!"

"I vote that we rub them down and then cool ourselves off over at TD's with an ice cream," suggested Lisa Atwood, running a dandy brush over Prancer's damp withers.

"That's a great idea!" Stevie said. "I'm amazed I didn't think of it first."

"Actually, Stevie, we're amazed you didn't think of it first, too," Carole laughed.

The girls continued to groom their horses. Stevie loosened Belle's leg wraps while Carole and Lisa gave Starlight and Prancer a good brushing.

"You know, it's too bad Max doesn't have one of those electronic horse groomers," Stevie said as she brushed Belle's thick mane.

"An electronic horse groomer?" Lisa frowned.

"Yeah. Remember that thing Judy used on Danny? It looked like a little vacuum cleaner," explained Stevie.

"Oh, right," said Carole. "But I can't help wondering how the horse feels about being treated like a piece of carpet."

"I don't know," Stevie said, chuckling. "But Judy loved it! And Danny didn't seem to mind."

"There you three are!" A woman's excited voice rang out from the far end of the stable.

The girls turned. Deborah Hale, Max Regnery's wife, hurried toward them, their baby girl, Maxi, in her arms. "Max said you had just finished the advanced jumps class and were probably on your way to TD's. I'm so glad I caught you!"

"What's up, Deborah?" Lisa shot a puzzled glance at Stevie and Carole.

Deborah spoke in a rush. "I just got a call from Bart Charles, an editor down at the paper. He wants me to write a feature article, but first I need to go into the city to meet with him this afternoon. I can't take Maxi with me, and Max has three private lessons this afternoon, so I was wondering if you girls could help me out and sit with Maxi." She looked at The Saddle Club pleadingly.

"Sure." Carole answered for all of them without hesitation. "We'd be glad to."

"After all, that's what The Saddle Club is for—to help each other out whenever we need it." Stevie grinned. "And, Deborah, you and Maxi and Max are all honorary Saddle Club members."

"Wonderful," Deborah said with relief. "I'll go home and get ready. You guys come on over when you finish with your horses. Maxi and I will be waiting." Smiling happily, she hurried with Maxi out of the cool, dark stable and into the bright summer day.

After the girls finished grooming their horses, they put them back in their stalls with an extra armload of hay and walked over to the white clapboard farmhouse where Max and Deborah lived. It was up a slight hill just behind the stable. Deborah and Maxi were sitting in the wide porch swing, waiting for them.

"I can't tell you how much I appreciate this." Deborah smiled. She'd changed out of her jeans and was wearing a blue business suit that matched her eyes.

3

"It'll be fun," said Lisa.

"Well, just remember, Maxi's crawling now, and anything she can pick up goes immediately into her mouth. She ought to be ready for her nap in a little while, so this should be pretty easy baby-sitting. If you have any problems, though, just run down to the stable. Max and Mrs. Reg are both there and can help in an emergency." Deborah handed Maxi to Carole and checked her watch. "I've got to go! Thanks so much, girls. I'll see you in a couple of hours."

"Good luck!" Stevie called as Deborah ran to her car. "Don't worry about a thing."

"Ouch, Maxi! Let go!" Carole yelped. Maxi had grabbed one of Carole's small stirrup-shaped earrings and was trying to put it into her mouth. "I need that ear for the rest of summer vacation!"

"Come to Aunt Stevie, Maxi." Stevie held out her arms and tried to distract the baby from Carole's ear. Maxi gurgled, let go of the earring, and allowed Stevie to take her. Stevie began walking her up and down the porch, but stopped when Maxi grabbed a fistful of her long honey blond hair.

"Ow, Maxi!" Stevie cried. "That hair was attached to my head!" Maxi giggled and pulled even harder.

"Why don't we put her in her playpen?" Lisa suggested. "Deborah said it was almost time for her nap."

4

"Good idea," said Stevie, wincing with pain as Maxi yanked another handful of hair. "Otherwise I might wind up bald."

Lisa held the door open while Stevie carried Maxi into the house. Her playpen was set up in the living room. After Carole cleared it of a stuffed Big Bird and a plastic ball, Stevie laid Maxi down on her stomach. Immediately the baby rolled over and sat up, but Stevie and Lisa and Carole had already begun to tiptoe toward the kitchen.

"It's time for you to take a nap now, Maxi," Carole whispered as Maxi blinked. "Don't worry. We'll be right in here."

The girls gently closed the door and sat down at the kitchen table.

"How can we tell what's she doing in there if we're sitting in here?" Stevie frowned with concern.

"Haven't you ever seen one of these?" Lisa switched on a white plastic box that looked like a small radio.

"No," replied Stevie. "I don't baby-sit all that much. My last job was feeding Mrs. Perkins's parakeets."

Lisa smiled. "Well, this is even better than an electronic horse groomer. This is a baby monitor." She turned the dial. "Listen."

The girls bent over and listened to the monitor. They heard a slight rustling noise.

5

"Sounds like she might be getting comfortable to go to sleep," said Carole. "I wish my CD player sounded that clear."

"I wish my CD-ROM sounded like anything at all," complained Stevie. "I was up to the final level of that game Squelch when stupid Chad crashed the hard drive. Now the only thing the computer can say is 'You have performed an illegal operation. . . .' "

"Shhh!" Lisa said suddenly. "Listen."

The girls leaned over the monitor again. The gentle rustling noise had stopped. They heard a little chirp, then a louder whimper, and then a full-fledged cry.

"Come on," Lisa said as she got up from her chair. "Let's go calm her down and maybe we can get her to go to sleep."

The girls trooped back into the living room. Maxi was sitting up in her playpen, huge tears rolling down her cheeks. She lifted her arms to be picked up.

"Poor baby Maxi," Lisa said as she scooped up the child. "Let's put you in your chair swing and see if that makes you sleepy."

Lisa buckled Maxi into her swing while Stevie wound the motor.

"You know about chair swings, Stevie?" Carole asked with a laugh.

"Sure I do," replied Stevie. "My mom just sold my old one at a garage sale."

The girls sat and watched as the swing rocked Maxi back and forth. Slowly her eyelids began to droop, but then, as soon as she realized she was falling asleep, she jerked her head up and began to cry all over again.

"I don't think the swing is working," said Stevie as Maxi's sobs grew louder.

"Maybe some music would help," Carole suggested. She jumped up and began thumbing through some CDs that were stacked on a bookcase. She pulled one from the pile. "Here's a good one. *Beethoven, Bach, and the Glorious Sounds of Nature.*"

Carole put the CD into the player and turned up the volume. Suddenly the room was filled with a pipe organ blaring through the sounds of a summer storm. Maxi jumped straight up at the first clap of thunder and then started yowling more loudly than ever.

"Cut the music!" Lisa said, wide-eyed. "It's scaring her to death!" She unbuckled Maxi from the chair swing and held her in her arms. Maxi's face was red with rage, and she was hiccuping as well as crying. Lisa frowned at Stevie and Carole. "Don't just stand there! Think of something we can do to calm her down!"

"I know!" Stevie cried. "Let's show her a video!" She knelt down in front of the TV and rummaged through a stack of videotapes. "Here's one!" she said. "Cartoons. That should work fine."

Stevie slid the tape into the VCR, and with Lisa

7

holding Maxi, they all huddled in front of the TV to watch. Maxi quit crying as a pink elephant waltzed across the screen, but instead of growing sleepy, she started laughing and clapping her hands.

After a few minutes of the elephant's dance, Stevie looked over at Maxi. The baby's eyes were clear and bright. "This tape is great for cheering her up," she said, "but it sure isn't helping to put her to sleep."

They were watching another video when the front door opened. Deborah appeared in the living room, little wisps of red hair escaping from the bun at the base of her neck. "Hi, everybody," she called. "How's it going?"

The Saddle Club and Maxi rose from in front of the TV.

"Deborah!" Stevie said as Maxi held out her arms to her mother. "We're so glad you're back."

Deborah laughed and grinned at Maxi. "Are you having too much fun to take a nap, sugar?" she asked. She held Maxi close for a moment and smiled at her frazzled-looking baby-sitters. "Why don't you girls get something to eat? There's pizza in the freezer. Nuke it in the microwave while I take Maxi to her room and see if I can get her to sleep."

Deborah whirled Maxi down the hall while The Saddle Club retreated to the kitchen. By the time they had microwaved the pizza, Deborah had returned. "There," she said as she switched the baby monitor from the living room to Maxi's room. "She's sleeping like the proverbial baby."

"You're kidding." Stevie almost dropped the slice of pizza that was halfway to her mouth.

"No." Deborah smiled. "She seemed glad to get into her little crib."

"We tried to get her to sleep," Lisa explained as Deborah opened a big bottle of soda for everyone, "but nothing seemed to help."

"Right," said Carole. "We tried the baby swing, the Beethoven CD, and finally cartoons. We were about to run out of stuff to try."

"Since they've got electronic horse groomers, what they need to invent now is an electronic baby soother," Stevie said. "Life is tough enough without having to deal with all that crying."

Deborah shook her head and chuckled.

"What so funny?" cried Stevie. "I think a baby-soothing machine is a great idea!"

"Oh, it is, Stevie." Deborah nodded. "It just reminded me of the meeting I was in."

"Oh?" said Carole. "What was your meeting about?"

"About doing an article on the pioneers who crossed the prairies in covered wagons. If you think things are tough without a baby-soothing machine, you should have seen what traveling with a baby was like over a hundred years ago."

9

"That's true, but what's the big deal?" said Stevie. "I mean, that's the way people had to live back then. Today we've got computers and microwaves and televisions."

Deborah took some pizza for herself. "Actually, we still do have covered wagons today. I just met with the travel editor of my paper. He wants me to fly out West and go on a wagon train reenactment, then write an article about it."

"Neat," said Carole.

Deborah chewed her pizza thoughtfully. "Somebody recommended me, because they figured Max Regnery's wife must know a lot about horses. On the way home I decided that I should probably turn this assignment down, because my background isn't in horses, but maybe I was too hasty. After all, it's not important for me to be savvy about animals and the environment, as long as I'm with someone who is."

"Yes," Lisa said. "Max knows a lot about animals."

Deborah grinned at the girls. "Actually, I wasn't thinking about Max. He can't take time away from the stable right now. I was thinking about you guys. How would The Saddle Club like to go West? You know all about horses. It's a weeklong trip, and the newspaper will pay for a family of four. Maxi's too young to go, but I've got plenty of time to line up a baby-sitter. Sound like anything you'd be interested in?"

"Oh, boy!" cried Stevie. "Would we ever!"

"Count me in," Carole added with a grin. "I'd love to see if I'm as tough as the old trailblazers."

"I'd love to go, too," said Lisa. "But the toughest trail I'll have to blaze will be convincing my mother to let me be a modern-day pioneer."

"THIS SHOULD BE IT!" Stevie cried as she lunged across her bed to answer the phone for the fifteenth time that night. After The Saddle Club had left Deborah and Maxi, each girl had scurried home to ask her parents' permission to go on the wagon train reenactment. There had been flurries of phone calls among Deborah, the Hansons, the Atwoods, and the Lakes. Slowly, the details were explained and the permissions were granted. Carole could go. Stevie could go. But they were still waiting to hear from the last holdout, Mrs. Atwood.

"Oh, please say she said yes," Stevie said into the phone without bothering to say hello.

12

"She said yes!" Lisa's voice came through the receiver. "It took some real convincing, but she finally said okay."

"All right!" cried Stevie. "Now The Saddle Club can go on the Oregon Trail!"

"Won't it be fun?" replied Lisa. "I can hardly wait. I've got so much to do I'd better get off the phone. It seems like I've been talking all night."

"I know what you mean." Stevie massaged her left ear. "I've got lots to do, too. I'll call you first thing tomorrow."

Stevie hung up the phone, tired of talking but glad that both her best friends were going out West with her. It would be their best vacation ever. She leaped off her bed. A trip down the Oregon Trail was something she could really gloat about in front of Chad. She had just opened her bedroom door to go find him when the phone rang again.

"Oh, please!" she said as she leaped onto the bed again. "Hello?" she answered hurriedly.

A husky, nonfemale voice came over the phone. "Hi, Stevie. This is Phil."

"Oh, hi, Phil," Stevie replied more softly. "How are you?"

"I'm good. What on earth is going on? Your line's been busy for hours."

"Oh, just some Saddle Club plans to work out."

Stevie twisted the telephone cord around her finger. "What's up with you?"

"Well, something great just happened. About a month ago my dad made reservations for the whole family to go on a white-water rafting trip down the Colorado River. We were all set to go until yesterday, when my sister got this summer job that she's been dying to have. Now she wants to stay here with friends and work while we go on our trip. That leaves one space that's been reserved and will have to be paid for. I was wondering if you'd like to come with us. My mom and dad said it would be okay."

"That sounds wonderful!" Visions of paddling through rapids of foamy white water flashed through Stevie's mind. "I'd love to! But I'll have to ask my parents."

"I know. Get a pencil and I'll give you all the details."

"Okay. Hang on." Stevie searched frantically around her room for a pencil, finally finding a short, stubby one under her bed. A wadded-up piece of notebook paper was under the bed as well, so she smoothed it out and used it to scribble down Phil's information.

"This sounds really neat, Phil. I'm so glad you invited me. As soon as I get some kind of semiofficial answer from my parents, I'll call you back."

"I sure hope they say yes, Stevie," Phil said.

"Oh, I do, too. I'll talk to you soon!"

Stevie hung up the phone and looked at the notes she'd scrawled on the paper. Something seemed vaguely familiar about the dates, but she couldn't quite place it. Finally it hit her. Phil was going rafting at exactly the same time she had just promised to go on the Oregon Trail!

"Oh no," she said, her fingers automatically dialing Carole's number. "This is terrible."

"You'll never guess what just happened," Stevie blurted out as soon as Carole answered the phone.

"Your parents took back their permission for the Oregon Trail because you did something awful to Chad." Carole had known Stevie to get in trouble like this on more than one occasion.

"No, nothing like that. Phil just called and invited me to go with his family on a white-water rafting trip on exactly the same dates as the wagon train."

"Oh no!" said Carole. "That's terrible. Are you positive the dates are the same?"

"Yes," Stevie replied miserably, studying her scribbled notes. "I'm looking at them right here in black and white. They fly out West on Monday, then start rafting on Tuesday. Just think, Carole, it would be rafting with Phil and camping along the way and having a great time!"

Carole sighed. "That's a tough call, Stevie. Phil's trip

15

sounds wonderful, but don't forget that you did promise to do the wagon train trip, and Deborah is counting on all three of us."

"I know," replied Stevie.

"Plus, the newspaper is paying for the Oregon Trail trip. Wouldn't your parents have to pay for your part of Phil's trip?"

"Yes, they would."

"Well, Stevie, there's your answer. No parent would pay for an expensive rafting trip when you have another equally fabulous trip waiting for you for free."

"I hadn't thought of it that way, but you're right." Stevie knew her parents were generous, but she also knew that money was always tight in a family of four children.

"Anyway," Carole continued, "who says it might not be a good thing for you and Phil to be apart for a while?"

"What do you mean?" asked Stevie.

"You know that old saying 'absence makes the heart grow fonder'? You'll have plenty to do on the wagon train trip, but if all Phil's doing is paddling down a river, he might begin to think about you a lot."

"Think so?" Stevie pictured Phil pulling a paddle through the Colorado River, all the while seeing her face on the sunlit boulders, in the foamy white water, in the blue sky above.

16

"Yes," said Carole. "He might come back a totally different person."

"Well, I don't know that I want him to be totally different, but a little different might be okay," Stevie said with a smile. "I think you're right, Carole. I think it would be crazy for me not to go on a totally free, totally neat trip. Plus it might be the best thing in the world for Phil and me. I'm going to call him back right now and tell him!"

Stevie hung up the phone and dialed Phil's number. His sister answered; then Phil came on the line.

"Hi, Phil, this is Stevie."

"Hi, Stevie. Did you ask your parents about the trip?"

"Well, no. Actually, after we hung up I realized that your trip is scheduled at exactly the same time as a trip I promised to go on with The Saddle Club."

"What kind of trip?"

"It's a wagon train reenactment along the Oregon Trail. Max's wife, Deborah, is writing an article about it for the paper, and since Max can't go and we know all about horses, the paper is paying our way to go along with her."

"Didn't you know about this trip when I called before?" Phil sounded annoyed.

"Yes, but I didn't realize the dates were the same. I'm sorry. I've talked to so many people on the phone tonight, I just got mixed up."

17

"That's too bad, Stevie. I was really looking forward to you coming along. Now my little sister will get to invite her best friend, Sarah Groom."

Stevie frowned. "So what's wrong with Sarah Groom? She's a neat little kid."

"Yeah. Well, she's a neat little kid who's got this weird crush on me. Every time I say anything to her she just turns red and starts sighing."

Stevie laughed. "Gee, Phil, it must be pretty tough to have all these younger women throwing themselves at you."

"Stevie, you know that's not what I mean," Phil said.

"I know. I was just teasing. I really wish I could go on this trip with you, but I promised Deborah that I would go with her first, and a promise is a promise." Stevie smiled and coiled the telephone cord around her finger again. "Anyway, it might be good for us to take separate vacations."

"What do you mean?" Phil sounded surprised.

"I mean, you know how sometimes when you're away from a person you really like, you can begin to see them differently and it makes you realize how much you like them all over again? In fact, it makes you like them even better?"

"Yeah, I suppose," Phil admitted.

"Well, just think. By the time we both get back from

18

our vacations, we'll really have missed each other and we'll like each other all the more!"

Phil sighed. "I guess you're right, Stevie. But I still wish you were coming with us instead of Sarah."

"I do, too, Phil. But think of how great it'll be when we finally get back together!"

On that they said good-bye; then Stevie immediately dialed Carole and Lisa on three-way calling.

"I solved my Phil problem," Stevie announced proudly.

"How?" Lisa asked. "Carole just called and told me that he had asked you to go rafting at the same time as our wagon train trip."

"Well, first I explained to him that I'd promised you guys and Deborah first and that I had just gotten con-fused on the dates."

"What did he say?" asked Carole.

"He was real disappointed, because that meant his little sister would get to invite her best friend, Sarah Groom, who has a big crush on Phil."

"Uh-oh," said Lisa.

"No, it's okay," Stevie assured her. "Phil thinks Sarah is a pest. And anyway, I convinced Phil that the best thing in the world for us would be to be apart for a few days. We can see new sights and meet new people, and when we get back home we'll appreciate each other all the more."

"Did he believe that?" Lisa asked.

"He seemed to," replied Stevie. "Anyway, *I* think it's a great idea. Just think of all the new people we'll meet. Why, maybe you and Carole will meet some terrific guys on the wagon train."

"We might, Stevie," Carole laughed, "but so might you!"

"Me?" Stevie asked incredulously. "I don't think so."

"You never know!" teased Lisa.

Stevie started to reply, but a thought stopped her cold. She didn't think it would be possible for her to meet anybody half as cute and funny as Phil, but it was entirely possible that Phil might meet somebody a whole lot cuter and funnier than she was. And not just Sarah Groom. Lots of different people went on those rafting trips. What if some really cute girl fell out of her raft? Phil would leap in the river and rescue her and then their eyes would meet and they would fall—

"Stevie, are you still there?" Lisa's voice crackled over the phone.

"Huh?" Stevie pushed the thought of Phil and the cute half-drowned girl to the back of her mind. "Yes, I'm still here."

"Can you go to the mall with Deborah and us tomorrow? We need to get some supplies for the trip."

"Sure. What time?"

"Deborah said Max could watch Maxi at noon. Let's meet at the stable at about eleven-thirty."

"Sounds good to me," said Carole. "I'll see you two there tomorrow."

"Bye, Carole; bye, Lisa. See you tomorrow," Stevie said. She hung up the phone and massaged her ear again. The vision of Phil and the cute girl popped back into her head, but she ignored it. "Travel broadens your horizons," she told herself resolutely. "And if Phil's horizons are getting broadened, then mine will just have to be, too."

"WHICH STORE DO we want to do first?" Carole asked as she followed Deborah, Stevie, and Lisa into the mall. "I need a couple of pairs of socks."

"I could use some socks, too," said Stevie. She sniffed the air, then turned toward one corner of the mall, where the aroma of baking cookies rose from a small storefront café. "I could also use a large chocolate macadamia nut cookie."

"Let's get our shopping done first," Lisa said. "Then we can pig out on cookies."

"Did anybody bring a list?" asked Deborah.

Stevie and Carole shook their heads, but Lisa gave Deborah a resigned smile. "I did. Or at least my mother sent my packing list along. I don't need to buy that much on it." She reached in her purse for a sheet of paper. On it was a typed list of supplies Mrs. Atwood wanted Lisa to take.

"My mother is afraid that the nights will be cold. So she thinks I should take three sweaters, a down jacket, a heavy-duty sleeping bag with two extra blankets, two pillows, three sets of gloves, three sets of long underwear, moisturizing sunscreen, and a pair of earmuffs."

"Earmuffs?" Stevie frowned. "Where are you going to buy earmuffs in June?"

Lisa squinted at her list. "Actually, I already have earmuffs and most of the other things on this list. I just have to buy what my mother's typed an asterisk beside." She looked at her friends, then turned the page over and continued. "Then I have to get aspirin, bandages, cough syrup, decongestant, antihistamine, vitamins, and throat lozenges." She shrugged. "She thinks I might catch a cold."

"And I think you'll be suffering from exhaustion if you pack all that stuff," said Carole.

"Wait a minute." Deborah stopped in the middle of the mall. "Lisa, I know your mother wants to take good care of you, but I don't think she understands the nature of a wagon train reenactment. This is not going to be a cushy trip. We're really going to be traveling by covered wagon. We'll be responsible for all of our clothes and provisions ourselves. Unless you can fit all these things into a single backpack that you can carry, you're going to have to leave a lot of things along the trail."

Lisa blinked. "Along the trail?"

"Yes. It's going to be just like the old days, and the old days were awfully rough. People had to trash treasured items they brought from back East because they couldn't get them through the mud or over the mountains. It wasn't uncommon to see horsehair sofas and dining room tables and even pianos abandoned by the side of the trail."

"Wow," said Carole, her dark eyes wide with wonder.

Deborah went on. "We're going to have to travel light. I mean *really* light. Here's the list they faxed me." She unfolded a single sheet of paper. A short list of supplies covered the top half of the page, with the instructions in big capital letters: ALL YOUR SUPPLIES MUST FIT INTO ONE LARGE BAG.

"Gosh," Stevie said. "They aren't kidding. But why do we have to take laundry soap?"

Deborah laughed. "Because the directors of this trip want us to live as closely as possible to the lives the settlers lived. That means we'll be wearing pioneer clothing and washing both our clothes and ourselves in creeks along the way. No showers, no bathrooms, no hot water." She smiled at the girls' open mouths. "This

24

trip is to be as authentic as possible without endangering the participants."

"Cool," said Stevie.

"Sounds fun to me," agreed Carole.

"I'm all for it, too," said Lisa. "But we can't tell my mother. She'll never let me go if I don't take everything on this list with me."

The girls frowned for a moment, thinking. Then Stevie grinned. "I know what we can do. Let your mother pack all this stuff for you, and then you can bring it over to my house and stash it there during the trip. That way your mother'll think you've taken everything, and you can take only what you need."

"Would your mom mind?" Lisa asked.

Stevie shook her head. "We'll put your suitcases in my closet. My mom's afraid to go in my closet." She shrugged. "For that matter, everybody's afraid to go in my closet."

Carole laughed. "Why am I not surprised?"

Deborah raised one eyebrow at the giggling girls. "I know this sounds like a lot of fun to you guys now, but are you sure you can do without your computer games and your CDs and your VCRs for a whole week?"

"Sure we can," said Carole. "This is a real adventure instead of just goofy fake cyber-stuff."

"Okay." Deborah smiled. "Just wanted to be sure we were all on the same page here." She held up the short list of supplies again. "So who needs what from this list?"

The girls peered at the paper. "I've got all of that stuff at home," said Stevie. "Except the biodegradable soap."

"Me too," Lisa said.

"Me three," added Carole. "But I still need to buy some socks."

"Well, I think we can get the soap at the sporting goods store, which is down that way." Deborah pointed past the café. "I'm sure they have socks there, too."

They walked down to the sporting goods store, passing a computer software outlet and a music shop along the way.

Stevie gazed at a giant software display. "I wonder if they have the new version of Squelch."

"I don't know," replied Carole. "I was kind of wondering if the music store had the new Shimmery Emery CD." She stopped for an instant, then shook her head. "Stevie, what are we talking about? The day after tomorrow we're going to be living in a world without computers or CD players or anything."

Stevie grinned sheepishly. "I know, but we'll be back in a week. Should be a real challenge, huh?"

At the sporting goods store, Stevie and Carole found socks they liked, and everybody grabbed a big plastic bottle of liquid peppermint soap. They were standing in line to check out when Stevie heard a voice behind her.

"Hey, Stevie!"

She turned. Phil and his father stood there with a half-filled shopping cart.

"Hi, Phil. Hi, Mr. Marsten." She walked over to talk to them.

Phil's father smiled. "What are you doing here, Stevie? I figured you made most of your purchases at the tack shop."

"Oh, we had to get some biodegradable soap for our wagon train trip. We're going to be washing our clothes in creeks along the way."

Phil eyed the bottle Stevie held up. "Your trip sounds really neat, Stevie. You'll be like real pioneers."

"That's right." Stevie looked over at the Marstens' cart. It was filled with a cookstove, sleeping bags, and a cooler. "Looks like you're going to be taking a pretty neat trip yourself, Phil." She smiled at him. "I'm sorry it didn't work out that we could be together."

"I'm sorry, too. It would have been lots of fun."

Something caught Stevie's eye over Phil's shoulder. On a sale table near the cash register was a display of trip journals—little red plaid books of blank pages to write in. "Hey!" she cried. "I've got a great idea! Let's each get one of these and keep a diary of our trip. Then, when we get back home, we can share them with each

27

other. It'll be like writing one long letter full of all the interesting stuff we might forget."

"That is a great idea." Phil turned around and grabbed two journals off the shelf. He handed one to her. "One for you and one for me. That way I'll learn all about the Oregon Trail and you'll learn all about white-water rafting. It's almost like going on two vacations."

"Well, almost, but not quite." Stevie laughed. "Look, I've got to go. I hope you have a wonderful trip, Phil."

Phil gave her a gentle smile. "Same here, Stevie. I'll call you as soon as I get back to town." He waved to Lisa and Carole. "Have a great vacation! I'm sure the Oregon Trail will never be the same!"

"Thanks, Phil," called Carole. "Hope you have a good vacation, too."

Stevie waved to Phil, then rejoined her friends at the checkout line. After they had paid for their supplies, they walked slowly toward the entrance of the mall. Again the scent of fresh-baked cookies wafted through the air.

"I have a suggestion," said Stevie.

"I bet it has something to do with those cookies," Lisa laughed.

"Well, kind of. Since we're leaving the day after tomorrow, and since tomorrow we'll be busy packing and taking our last horseback ride at Pine Hollow, I vote we each get a cookie and drink a toast to our last contact with the modern world."

"Stevie, you can't drink a toast with a cookie," Carole said.

"Yeah, but we can click our cookies together before we take our first bite. That'll be just as good as a toast."

"Actually, I think that's a terrific idea," said Deborah. "They certainly won't be delivering any warm chocolate macadamia nut cookies on the Oregon Trail!"

"THERE!" STEVIE SHOVED Lisa's last suitcase into the back of her closet. "Safe and sound. Two suitcases all hidden away for your vacation."

"Are you sure your mother won't find these and call my mother?" Lisa's blue eyes clouded with worry as she stuffed the last of her supplies into a single duffel bag.

"Absolutely." Stevie pointed to her closet. "Would you willingly look for something in there if you didn't desperately need it?"

Carole and Lisa gazed at the jumbled array of books, shoes, clothes, papers, and old school projects that spilled from the closet.

"I think you're safe, Lisa." Carole's easy laugh was reassuring. "Even if Mrs. Lake were looking for your luggage, she probably couldn't find it for a couple of weeks, anyway."

"Hey, Stevie!" Stevie's brother Chad yelled from the living room. "Max and Deborah are here."

"All right!" Stevie grabbed her backpack. "Westward ho, pioneers!"

The girls said good-bye to the Lakes, then piled into the Pine Hollow van. "How's everybody doing this afternoon?" Max asked as he turned toward the airport. "Are you guys ready to rough it?"

"We sure are." Carole smoothed her long dark hair back behind her ears.

"And are you fully aware of how much you'll be expected to work during this trip?" Deborah asked from the front seat.

"Don't worry," answered Stevie. "We've worked real hard at the Devines' dude ranch. And we've had a lot of experience in riding Western."

Deborah frowned. "Well, don't forget you'll be riding Western in authentic costumes. Hats, bonnets, skirts."

"Skirts?" A note of alarm rose in Stevie's voice.

"Yes. Skirts. The whole nine historically correct yards."

"Will we have to ride sidesaddle?" Lisa asked.

31

"Good question," Deborah replied. "I don't know. I know we'll all be assigned roles to play, where we'll assume the lives of people who actually might have gone along the trail. That's done at Plimoth Plantation and a lot of other historic sites."

"Cool." Stevie fluttered her eyelashes. "Maybe they'll let me be somebody famous, like that opera singer, Jenny Lind."

Lisa shook her head. "Stevie, they'll be more likely to typecast you as Calamity Jane."

An hour later, they all said good-bye to Max and Maxi and boarded the plane that would take them out West. "This is so cool," Carole breathed as the plane gathered speed and hurtled down the runway. "If I weren't so crazy about horses, I'd be crazy about flying."

"Then we'd have to change the name of our club," said Lisa. "We'd have to be something like The Silver Wings Club instead of The Saddle Club."

"That might be neat," Stevie said, looking out the window as the landscape rushed by. "But I don't think it would be as much fun."

Just as the sun was disappearing behind the mountains, their plane landed in what looked like a wide patch of Western prairie. Deborah hailed one of the few taxis available at the small regional airport, and soon they were deposited in front of a rambling old hotel called the Wagon Train Lodge.

"Wow," Carole said as Deborah paid the cabdriver. "Let's go look at all the covered wagons parked by the corral!"

"Let's get signed in first, girls." Deborah laid a hand on Carole's shoulder. "Then we can check out the wagons."

They carried their bags into a large, airy lobby where stuffed buffalo and moose heads lined the wall. Whole families of other Oregon Trail trekkers bustled around the room, and Deborah and the girls had to take a place at the end of a long check-in line.

"Yes, ma'am?" the clerk said when they finally reached the front desk.

"We're the Hale party from Willow Creek, Virginia. We have reservations on Wagons West."

"Ah, yes." The clerk looked at his computer screen. "You're in the Kit Carson Suite. Fourth floor, three doors to the right of the elevator." He handed two keys to Deborah. "It's our policy to remind all our Wagons West folks that breakfast and the first orientation meeting start at five-thirty sharp, so we advise an early bedtime."

"Five-thirty in the morning?" Stevie gulped.

The clerk nodded at Stevie and smiled at Deborah. "Shall I have your luggage sent to your room? That way you and the girls can have a chance to look around the corral before dark."

"Thanks," Deborah said. "That would be great."

They left their bags with the clerk and went back outside to get a closer look at the wagons, whose white canvas covers resembled oddly shaped ghosts in the growing darkness.

"Wow," said Stevie as she touched one of the wooden wheels. "I can't believe I'm actually touching a real covered-wagon wheel."

"I can't get over how rickety they look," said Lisa. "Can you imagine people actually packing all their possessions in one wagon and crossing rivers and prairies and mountains in it?"

Carole ran her hand along the rough canvas top of the wagon. "I wonder what they did when it got cold? This canvas doesn't look like it would be much protection from the wind and rain."

"You've got to admire the pioneers' bravery," said Deborah, staring at the wagon. "It took a lot of courage to do what they did." She smiled at the girls in the dim light. "But right now, we need to have the courage to go to bed. Five-thirty is going to come awfully early!"

They trooped back into the lodge and took the elevator up to the fourth floor. The Kit Carson Suite had two rooms, each with two double beds.

Deborah took one room for herself. "I'm going in here to call Max and let him know we arrived okay, and then I'm going to hit the sack. I'll see you three bright and early in the morning."

"Okay, Deborah," said Lisa and Carole. "Good night."

"I know you're excited, but try to get some sleep, girls. You'll need to be wide awake tomorrow."

"We will," promised Stevie.

A few minutes later, the lights were out and everyone was in bed.

"I still can't believe we're actually here," said Stevie. "Just think! Real wagons crossing the prairie to settle the West, just like they did over a hundred years ago! Cowboys, cattle rustlers, gold miners, and sodbusters!"

"Go to sleep, Stevie," said Carole.

"I can't. I'm too excited."

"You have to, Stevie. Otherwise we'll all be dead tomorrow."

"You're right." Stevie flopped back down in bed. "I promise I won't talk anymore. I just hope I can go to sleep."

"Close your eyes and count backward from a hundred," said Lisa, her voice already sounding groggy. "That always works for me."

Stevie closed her eyes. "Ninety-nine," she said to herself. "Ninety-eight . . . ninety-seven . . ."

Suddenly a loud clanging erupted in the room.

"What in the world?" Stevie sat up straight in bed, her heart pounding wildly. A funny gray light was pouring through the windows. She gasped. Was the lodge on fire?

"Lisa! Carole! Wake up!" Stevie cried, leaping out of bed and running over to the window. "I think we need to evacuate!"

She looked out the window and blinked. The funny gray light was not flames, but rather the first light of dawn coming over the mountains. And the noise she heard was not a fire alarm, but a man ringing a ranch-style triangle just below their window.

"Arggggh!" Stevie groaned. She turned back to Lisa and Carole, who were blinking at her sleepily. "Never mind. The lodge isn't on fire. This is just how they wake you up out here."

"Hi, girls!" Deborah breezed into their room, already dressed in jeans and a gingham shirt. "It's five-thirty. Time to rise and shine."

Deborah laughed as Carole and Lisa pulled the blankets back over their heads. "You guys should feel lucky. I read yesterday that the pioneer women had to get up at four o'clock to have breakfast ready by five-thirty. Think of how easy we have it! We get to sleep until almost five-thirty and breakfast is already waiting for us!"

36

A little while later, Stevie, Carole, and Lisa sat with all the other Oregon Trail trekkers at a long table, eating a gummy yellow corn cereal the waiters called mush.

"Is this what the pioneers ate?" Lisa whispered to Carole as she stirred the thick goop with her spoon.

"Must be," replied Carole. "I thought they ate bacon and eggs and things like that."

"It's not so bad," said Stevie, digging into her third bowl of the mush. "But of course, I'm starving."

Just then a tall, thin man with a salt-and-pepper beard came over. He wore a homespun blue shirt and a red bandanna tied around his neck. "Hi, girls," he said. "I'm Jeremy Barksdale, your wagon train leader. How do you like your breakfast?"

"It's all right," replied Stevie. "It's not Lucky Charms, but it will do."

Jeremy smiled. "Well, you know we like to make these trips authentic. Lucky Charms wasn't on the menu a hundred years ago. You're eating exactly the same thing as the pioneers."

"Yes, and Stevie's probably eating as much as the pioneers, too," said Carole, watching as Stevie polished off her third helping.

Stevie shrugged at Jeremy and her friends. "A girl's got to keep her strength up somehow."

As the trekkers continued their breakfasts, Jeremy walked over to a small platform and addressed the entire dining room.

"Hi, everybody." He held a microphone in one hand. "Welcome to Wagons West. I'm Jeremy Barksdale, and I'm your wagon train master. While you finish your breakfast, I'd like to fill you in on some historical details about the Oregon Trail and tell you some more about this trip."

He cleared his throat. "From the 1840s through the 1860s, nearly four hundred thousand pioneers crossed the western United States on what we call the Oregon Trail. It was dangerous—pioneers died from cold, hunger, cholera, and Indian attacks—and it was slow. It would take the pioneers a full week to travel the same distance we can travel by car in an hour or two today."

"Gosh," whispered Lisa. "I didn't know that."

"Despite the dangers, though, a lot of brave settlers drove these prairie schooners through knee-deep mud, raging rivers, and blinding dust storms all the way to Oregon." Jeremy smiled. "Today, I don't think we'll be in too much physical danger, but as much as possible, on Wagons West all of you will be living the authentic lives of the pioneers." He looked over his audience. "Are there any questions?"

A gray-haired man sitting in the back raised his hand. "Can you tell us about our itinerary?"

"Sure. For six days we'll travel and work just as hard as the pioneers did. At noon on the fourth day, we'll stop at Miller's Rock." He smiled knowingly at the audience. "I guarantee that by the time we stop at Miller's Rock, each of you will be a different person. You will have become the pioneers you've set out to learn about."

A murmur rippled through the crowd; then Jeremy continued. "At the end of the fifth day, we'll stop to rest at Clinchport. We'll have one day to rest up and then enjoy the rodeo going on there. Some of you may even want to participate in some of the events." He looked over the dining room. "How does that sound to everyone? Are you prepared for the challenge?"

"Sounds good to me," said Carole.

"Me too," agreed Stevie. "Although I seriously doubt we'll be turning into real pioneers."

When the dining room grew quiet again, Jeremy continued. "Now I'd like to ask each of you to introduce yourself to the group. You're going to get to know each other very well during the next six days." Jeremy looked at The Saddle Club table. "Why don't you ladies start us off?"

Deborah stood up. She had whispered to the girls before breakfast that she wasn't going to tell anybody that she was a reporter there on assignment.

"Hi, everybody." She smiled toward the other tables.

39

"My name is Deborah Hale and I'm from Willow Creek, Virginia. I'm taking my niece Lisa on this trip, and I'm chaperoning her and her two friends, Carole and Stevie."

Carole, Lisa, and Stevie stood and briefly introduced themselves. When they finished, Deborah stood up again. "All these girls," she added proudly, "modestly forgot to mention that they are excellent horsewomen."

"Thanks, ladies. That's great. We need all the excellent horsewomen we can get." Jeremy smiled. "Next?"

The introductions continued around the room. Sitting close to the girls were Mr. Cate, a bearded man from Alabama who played the harmonica, and Polly Shaver, a dance instructor from Ohio. There were families traveling with children younger than The Saddle Club girls and a few retired people on vacation. At one table across the room, though, a tall teenage boy arose.

"Hi, folks," he said. "My name is Gabriel. I'm also a horseback rider, and I've studied the Oregon Trail since I was in the fifth grade. I think it's terrific, the part men played in opening up the West for the future of America."

"What does he mean, *men?*" Stevie whispered to Carole and Lisa. "Women played just as important a part."

"He probably means *men* as in *people*," Carole said.

40

"Yeah, Stevie," Lisa assured her. "He means *men* in the generic sense."

Stevie was about to say something else, but she looked over and saw Deborah giving them the evil eye. Reluctantly she sat back in her seat and listened to the next introduction.

A pretty little girl with long blond hair was introducing herself. "Hi. My name's Eileen. I'm eight years old. I've been looking forward to coming on this trip for months, and I'm thrilled to be going with all of you. I just know we'll all have a wonderful time!"

Everyone laughed, then applauded Eileen's enthusiasm. The last few people introduced themselves; then Jeremy spoke again.

"Thanks, everybody. Not surprisingly, this group is much like the original groups that traveled the trails— about thirty people who range in age from children to grandparents and coming from all walks of life." He glanced at a small notebook he'd been scribbling in. "While you introduced yourselves, I took some notes, and now I'd like to assign everybody a role to play."

A murmur of anticipation went through the dining room.

Jeremy looked at The Saddle Club's table. "Since Deborah's already in charge of these three young ladies, I've decided that she can be an 1840s schoolmarm

41

who's adopted these three orphans. She's taught them their readin' and writin' and 'rithmetic, and she's taking her brood across the country to establish a school for girls in Oregon." Jeremy smiled at them. "You'll all be traveling in one wagon. Deborah, you and Stevie will drive. Carole, you'll ride a horse, and Lisa, you will be in charge of the cow."

"The cow?" Lisa's jaw dropped.

"Sure," Jeremy replied. "Our cook, Shelly Bean, has to have some way to take milk along the trail. We're not carrying any refrigerators, you know."

"Do I have to milk the cow?" asked Lisa.

Jeremy smiled. "No, Shelly will take care of the milking. You'll just have to make sure that the cow gets fed and watered and stays in good shape."

"Oh." Lisa sat back in her chair as Jeremy assigned the next people their roles. "When he said *authentic*, he wasn't kidding around."

"Shhh!" Stevie said suddenly as Jeremy pointed to Gabriel. "Let's hear what Mr. He-Man of the West gets to be!"

"Gabriel, since you're a rider and a great student of history, how about we make you assistant trail boss?"

Gabriel's face lit up with pride. "No problem," he said confidently. "I can handle that."

"I bet," scoffed Stevie. "He probably couldn't lead

42

this wagon train across the parking lot." She folded her arms across her chest. Then Jeremy began to speak again.

"Okay. Now that everyone's gotten a role, it's time to visit the clothes locker for your costumes and then start loading up your wagons. We're going to spend the rest of the day here at the lodge, practicing our roles and becoming accustomed to the lives we're going to be living. Then, tomorrow, it's wagons ho!" He grinned. "Good luck. And don't hesitate to holler if you need help."

Deborah and the girls rose from the table and decided to go outside and choose their wagon first. "This one looks good," said Carole, poking her head inside one that was parked under a tree. "At least I don't see any tears in the canvas where the rain could get in." She held up a horse collar. "Look, Stevie, here's the harness for the horses. Why don't you go find our team and hitch them up while Lisa and I get our costumes? We'll bring you something neat to wear."

"Okay," said Stevie. "Just don't bring me any goofy-looking old dress. I couldn't possibly drive this wagon in a skirt."

While Lisa and Carole went to get the costumes, Jeremy introduced Stevie to their team, two big bay quarter horses named Yankee and Doodle. Both walked docilely behind her as she led them back to the wagon. She had just begun to hitch them to the traces when she heard a voice behind her.

"Hey, I'll be happy to help you with that!"

Stevie turned. There, with a smug grin on his face, was Gabriel, Mr. Know-It-All since the fifth grade.

"Well, thanks, but I don't need any help with this," Stevie said as she pulled the breast collar over Doodle's head. She adjusted the collar and had to smile to herself when she saw how closely Gabriel was watching her.

"Looks like you've done that before," he said with some disappointment as Stevie slid the saddle onto Doodle's back and buckled the crupper under his tail.

"I have," replied Stevie. "Have you ever been an assistant trail boss before?"

"No." Gabriel folded his arms across his chest. "But I think I can handle it."

Stevie raised one eyebrow as she pulled the horse collar onto Yankee. "Well, if you need any help, feel free to call on me and my friends."

Gabriel gave a snide chuckle. "Thanks, but I don't think that's going to happen. Men didn't rely on the womenfolk to help them guide the wagon train."

"Yes, but the menfolk relied on women for a lot of other important jobs," said Stevie. "Like mending clothes and healing sick people and cooking meals."

She glared at Gabriel. "Maybe if you expect to eat anything on this trip, you ought to keep certain opinions to yourself."

Gabriel rolled his eyes. "Just my rotten luck," he muttered. "The first women's libber is going to Oregon on my wagon train."

"Maybe it's your *good* luck," Stevie whispered, hitching up Yankee and watching as Gabriel hurried over to help a family struggling with their horses' harness. "Now you can learn firsthand what womenfolk can really do!"

By late afternoon Stevie had shown Deborah how to steer their horses to the right by saying "gee" and to the left by calling "haw." Much to her disgust, she had also donned a long-sleeved brown dress that scratched every inch of her. Lisa was outfitted in an equally itchy blue dress with a floppy collar, while Carole, because she was a horse rider, sported a blue homespun shirt and jeans with a battered cowboy hat.

"I can't believe I have to drive this wagon across the country in a dress," Stevie complained, already scratching behind one shoulder. "Are you sure they didn't have any extra jeans?"

"I'm sure, Stevie," Carole explained for the third

46

time as she tried to relax on her new horse, a gray Appaloosa named Nikkia. "All the trousers were for the people who'd been assigned horses."

"I'll tell you something else you're not going to believe," called Lisa as she pulled a slow-moving white cow up to their wagon.

"What?" Stevie asked grumpily.

"This cow's name," Lisa replied.

"Let me guess," Carole said as Nikkia slapped his ears back and tossed his head. "Bossy."

"Better than that."

"Flossy," guessed Stevie, still scratching.

"Even better than that," Lisa said.

"Okay, we give up," said Carole.

"Veronica!" Lisa answered with a huge grin.

Stevie and Carole howled with laughter. Veronica di Angelo was the snobbiest, most stuck-up girl at Pine Hollow Stables. Somehow it was poetic justice that she should share her glamorous name with a stubborn cow.

"Veronica would just die if she knew someone had named a cow after her," hooted Stevie, forgetting about her scratchy dress.

"I know," Lisa laughed. "Isn't it great?"

A little while later it was time to corral the livestock for the night. Lisa took Veronica back to her pasture, while Carole gratefully pulled off Nikkia's heavy Western saddle. As Stevie began to unhitch Yankee and

Doodle, she noticed that Gabriel was leaning against a fence watching her work. For once his blue eyes sparkled in honest admiration at the smooth way she handled the horses. She was just about to say something to him when someone called him from the other end of the wagon train. She turned back to her horses, and as she returned them to the corral she realized that every time she'd seen Gabriel that day, he'd been going from wagon to wagon, pitching in wherever he was needed and generally giving people good advice.

"Well, okay, so he knows a lot," she admitted to Yankee and Doodle as they walked along beside her. "But his attitude toward 'the womenfolk' could sure be improved."

After the girls had taken care of their livestock, they decided to move from their comfortable lodge rooms out to their wagon. "If we're roughing it," said Stevie, "we ought to really rough it." Just as they were spreading their sleeping bags out on the hard wagon floor, the dinner bell rang.

"Howdy, pilgrims!" called a short, dumpy man with a grizzled beard. "My name's Shelly Bean and I'm the cook of this outfit. All who are eating out here with me need to come and get it now!"

"Let's go," said Stevie, scrambling out the back end of the wagon and nearly tripping over the hem of her long dress. "I'm starved!"

Everyone lined up. As they passed the chuck wagon, Shelly Bean grinned and ladled some odd-smelling stew onto their plates. Then they all sat in a big circle around the campfire.

"How do you like your supper?" Jeremy asked after everyone had begun to eat.

"Tastes kind of unusual," a woman said, coughing slightly.

"It's Shelly's special pemmican stew," Jeremy explained. "Dried meat and berries mixed in with cornmeal. The Cree Indians shared the recipe with the pioneers. It was a popular dish along this trail."

Everyone ate the stew. Though it was something they probably wouldn't have liked at home, here, because they were sitting around a fire in the open country and were tired from a hard day's preparation for their journey, it tasted fine.

"Are we going to be eating this every night?" someone asked Jeremy.

He shook his head. "No. We won't be lucky enough to have pemmican stew every night. Most of what we eat we'll be carrying with us, just like the pioneers. We'll be traveling the same route as them, as much as modern towns and highways permit. That means we won't have any electricity, running water, or heat. All we'll have is the outdoors and the challenge of nature."

Deborah looked guiltily over at the rucksack that

held her laptop computer. "I think I'd better leave that at the lodge," she whispered to the girls. "It won't do me any good anyway, without an outlet to recharge the batteries."

"I feel like I'm saying good-bye to the modern world forever," Lisa said, taking the last bite of her stew.

Jeremy spoke as if he'd read her mind. "Even though we're going to live the lives the pioneers lived as much as possible, I will have a cell phone, just in case of emergency. Anybody else here carrying a cell phone?"

Four people raised their hands.

"Good," said Jeremy. "We'll be well prepared. On our third night out we're scheduled to meet with some folks from a nearby dude ranch who are participating in a mock cattle drive. We'll have fresh food and a hoedown and a real celebration by the fire. It should be a lot of fun."

"It sounds terrific!" someone called from across the fire.

"I think you'll find the next six days will be an experience you won't soon forget," Jeremy said.

"I won't soon forget spending six days in this dumb dress," grumbled Stevie, trying to scratch between her shoulder blades.

After everyone had finished supper, Stevie, Carole, and Lisa helped wash the dishes. Then they sponged themselves off in the cold, rushing creek and walked slowly toward their wagon.

"I can't believe how tired I am, and it's not even sundown!" Carole said.

"I know." Lisa yawned. "That sleeping bag is going to feel great."

"I've got to write in my journal some before I go to sleep," Stevie said as the girls climbed into the back of the wagon.

"Are you sure you've got the energy for that?" Carole asked.

"Well, I am tired, but I made Phil a promise and I'm going to keep it."

The girls settled in next to Deborah, who was already in her sleeping bag. Stevie lit a small oil lamp and dug her pen and journal out of her backpack.

"Don't write too late, Stevie," said Deborah from under her covers. "Remember, the real journey starts tomorrow at sunup."

"I won't," Stevie whispered. She sat up and balanced the journal on her legs. *Day One*, she wrote at the top of the first page.

Today we had a breakfast of mush and met our wagon master, Jeremy Barksdale. We've also met our horses and our cow and one very stuck-up boy named

51

Gabriel, who thinks men conquered the West all by themselves.

Stevie started to write that Gabriel did know all about wagons and harnesses and packing supplies, but she decided Phil probably wouldn't be interested in that. Instead, she wrote:

Gabriel is tall and lean, with dark brown hair and deep blue eyes. Occasionally he will smile, and then he has a dimple in his right cheek.

"Oh no," Stevie whispered, feeling a hot blush of embarrassment as she read over her words. "I can't say that!" Quickly she tore the page out of her journal and started again.

Today we had a breakfast of mush and met our wagon master, Jeremy Barksdale. We've met our horses and our cow and one very stuck-up boy named Gabriel, who thinks men conquered the West all by themselves. He considers himself an expert on everything from wagon driving to sheepherding, but I wonder how much he really knows. It should be fun to see how well he does with his job of assistant trail boss.

52

Stevie reread her words and smiled. This was better. This was more like the real Gabriel. She added a few paragraphs about their wagon and the campfire; then she was done for the evening. She stuffed her journal back into her bag, blew out the lamp, and curled into her sleeping bag. In an instant she was asleep.

IT WAS A little past midnight when Deborah shook Carole and Lisa awake. "Girls, there's an emergency phone call for me at the lodge. You sit tight and I'll be back as soon as I can."

"Okay," Lisa mumbled, rubbing her eyes.

By the time Deborah had climbed over the sleeping bags and out of the wagon, all three girls were wide awake.

"What do you think it could be?" Carole asked as she watched Deborah and Jeremy hurry toward the lodge.

"I hope nothing's wrong with Maxi," said Stevie.

"Or Max," added Lisa.

For what seemed like forever, they huddled in the dark wagon, wondering what could have gone wrong. Finally Deborah reappeared.

"Okay, girls, here's the deal. My father was in a car accident this evening. He's in a hospital right now, and though it looks like he's going to be okay, my mom's really upset. Since I'm an only child, I have to be there for both of them. I hope you won't be too disappointed, but I'm afraid we'll have to leave right away."

"Sure, Deborah. We understand. We would want to be there if any of our parents were hurt," said Carole, trying to hide her disappointment.

"Jeremy's making our flight arrangements, so I guess the best thing for us to do is to pack our stuff up and go back to the lodge. I'm really sorry this had to happen."

"Don't worry about it, Deborah," said Lisa. "This would have been a great trip, but we can do it some other time."

"Thanks. I appreciate your understanding." Deborah gave a tired sigh.

They had just begun to roll up their sleeping bags when Jeremy appeared at the back of the wagon.

"Hey, Deborah, I was thinking. I watched these girls all day today and I think they're all extremely capable, mature young ladies. It would be a shame to have them come this far and then have to leave. Why don't you let me take them under my personal wing for the rest of the trip? That is, if it's okay with you."

Deborah blinked. "Well, it's okay with me if it's okay with them. And, of course, with their parents."

"It's okay with us," Stevie assured her.

"Well, let's go call everybody in Virginia and explain the situation."

An hour later, the girls stood with Deborah in the lobby of the lodge. They had all gotten permission from their parents to remain on the trip, and they were waiting with Deborah for the cab that was to take her back to the airport.

"It's too bad I'm not going to be able to write that article," Deborah said as she leaned against a long leather sofa. "That was the whole reason we came out here in the first place."

"Oh, don't worry about that, Deborah," Carole said. "Lisa and Stevie and I can do all the research you could possibly want. Stevie's even keeping a journal."

"That's right," said Stevie. "We can help you write the article when we get back."

Lisa gave Deborah a hug. "It's the least we can do."

"Well, thanks, girls," Deborah said, hugging each of them. "I appreciate your good intentions."

"No, really," insisted Stevie. "We can be a big help. I know we can."

Just then the cab pulled up.

"I've got to go," said Deborah, grabbing her backpack. "You girls be careful and do what Jeremy tells you. I'll see you in about a week!"

The Saddle Club waved as the cab pulled away from the lodge, leaving them standing alone with ten covered wagons under a dark sky spangled with stars.

6

"STEVIE! WAKE UP!" Carole reined in Nikkia and peered at Stevie, who was nodding in the driver's seat of the wagon. Breakfast was over, and everyone was waiting to pull out.

"I'm not asleep," Stevie said, yawning. "I'm just resting my eyes. I never could get back to sleep after Deborah left."

"Me neither," said Lisa, who stood on the other side of the wagon holding Veronica by a frazzled rope. Lisa rubbed her eyes. "I think I got about fifteen minutes of sleep the entire night. I couldn't believe it when the triangle rang at five-thirty. This is going to be one long day!"

Stevie blinked at Jeremy, who had ridden to the front of the column. Suddenly she sat up straight and tightened the reins. "I'm not sure, but I think our long day might be starting right now."

The girls looked toward the lead wagon. Jeremy, on a big brown-and-white paint horse, stood to one side of it. He waited for everyone's attention, then rose in his stirrups.

"Everyone ready?" he called, lifting his hat high above his head and grinning broadly.

Everyone in the wagon train cheered.

"Then wagons ho!" he called. His horse rose up once on its hind legs, then turned quickly around. With a swish of its tail, it carried Jeremy westward at a brisk trot. One by one, the wagons began to lumber after him.

"Here we go!" Stevie cried when their turn to move came. She popped Yankee and Doodle's reins. The horses strained hard against their collars. Then all at once The Saddle Club began to roll west.

The morning was a busy one. Stevie itched constantly from the rough material of her dress, and the wagon bumped her rear end with every turn of the wheels. The sun beamed down on the back of her neck, and though Yankee and Doodle pulled the wagon easily, they paid far more attention to the team in front of them than they did to Stevie.

Lisa spent the morning trying to control Veronica, who tended to stop every ten feet to graze leisurely by the side of the road.

"Come on, Veronica," Lisa would coo sweetly, giving a gentle tug on the rope. "We need to walk this way, over by the wagons." Veronica would look dully at Lisa, take one step, then pull up a mouthful of grass as the wagon train rolled past them. "Come on, sweet Veronica," Lisa would call again, tugging harder. Veronica would chew her grass and budge only an inch. Finally, as the dust from the passing wagons began to sting Lisa's eyes and clog her nose, she took a deep breath and gave a mighty heave on Veronica's rope. "Come on, you nitwit cow!" she commanded. At that, Veronica bawled a low *moo* and began to trudge forward.

Though she was sleepy, Carole was able to endure Nikkia's rough trot all morning. She could tell by the way the stocky Appaloosa slapped his ears back when she asked for a canter that he had been the victim of a lot of what she called kick-and-yank riders. As she looked around, she saw that many of the people riding with the wagon train were that kind of rider.

"If you pull the right rein gently, then release it, he'll go more willingly," she finally told Karen Nicely, a woman whose horse was so confused by her aids that he had just stopped, unable to figure out which way she wanted him to go.

"Thanks," Karen Nicely said, trying what Carole had suggested.

"Hey, how do you make them stop?" asked a breathless man whose horse was jigging sideways.

"And how do you make them back up?" called someone else.

Suddenly Carole found herself giving mini-riding lessons, right there in the middle of the trail. She didn't mind, because she didn't want any novice riders abusing their horses from lack of knowledge. Still, showing everybody what to do as the wagons rolled around them was exhausting. *I never realized before what a good job Max does of teaching,* she thought as she and Nikkia were finally able to canter back up to Stevie and the wagon.

They stopped for lunch at midday. Stevie pulled the team to a halt while Carole fetched water for Veronica and their three horses. Lisa tugged Veronica up to the wagon and tied her to the rear wheel. After they had taken care of their animals, they trudged over to the chow line.

"How's it going for you girls?" Jeremy asked as he strode past.

Stevie yawned. "Fine, except I've got blisters on my rear from the wagon, and blisters on my fingers from the reins, plus neither Yankee nor Doodle is paying me a whole lot of attention."

"And Veronica pays me no attention at all," added Lisa.

Jeremy grinned. "Great. This is exactly what the pioneers had to deal with—cranky cows and hardmouthed horses. You're getting a real taste of history!"

"Right now, I'd rather get a real taste of lunch!" said Carole as Jeremy ran over to assist a family whose wagon wheel needed to be greased.

Shelly Bean worked hard ladling out the fried cornmeal mush and fresh apples he'd fixed for lunch. "Eat hearty!" he called as the girls took their plates and sat down beside a small pond. The mush and apples seemed like a peculiar lunch, but they tasted wonderful, and soon they felt their usual energy levels returning.

"I'm beginning to understand why they assigned four people to a wagon," Stevie said, rubbing the blisters on her hand. "Taking care of a wagon plus three horses and a cow is a tough job for four people, let alone three."

"Don't forget that Jeremy is always here to help us," Carole said.

"Oh, I think we'll be fine, but it's exhausting doing all these jobs by ourselves." Lisa wiped the dust from her forehead. "Why don't we change places every few hours? The jobs won't get any easier, but at least we'll exercise different parts of our anatomies. Stevie, you won't get bounced so badly; Carole, your legs won't be so sore; and maybe one of you will have better luck with the cow."

"That's a good idea," agreed Stevie. "Although I don't think any of us would have much luck with anything named Veronica."

After lunch they resumed their jobs, agreeing to switch off in an hour. Stevie pulled on a pair of leather gloves she'd thrown into her backpack, so the blisters on her fingers bothered her less. Once again Jeremy rode to the head of the column, waved his hat, and shouted, "Wagons ho!" And once again they were off.

The wagons rolled westward onto the vast plains. Miles of flat, nearly treeless land stretched to the horizon. As far as the girls could see, the long green grass was dotted with small purple wildflowers. Little yellow birds Polly Shaver called western meadowlarks chattered to each other, and the delicious smell of earth and new grass drifted on the warm breeze.

"This doesn't look much like Virginia, does it?" Stevie commented as Lisa tugged Veronica along.

"No, but it's just as pretty." Lisa looked out over the prairie. "It's pretty in a flatter, more open way."

"I wonder how far away we can see." Carole squinted at the distant horizon from atop Nikkia's back.

"Maybe fifty miles," guessed Stevie. "After all, these are the wide-open spaces."

Suddenly Veronica stopped dead in her tracks. She twisted her head around and pulled up a mouthful of grass. "Looks like it's Veronica's snack time." Lisa shrugged at Stevie as the wagon rumbled past her. "We'll catch up to you later."

"Okay." Stevie scratched under the collar of her dress. "See you soon."

She and Carole rolled on until a voice came from the rear of the train. "Hey, Carole! Can you help me with this horse?"

Carole looked over her shoulder to see a desperate-looking man on an equally desperate-looking pinto waving at her. "I think someone needs a riding lesson," she said to Stevie as she turned Nikkia and began to trot toward the man. "I'll be back in a few minutes!"

"Don't teach him anything I wouldn't teach him!" warned Stevie with a laugh.

Stevie drove on, content to let the sun warm her face as Yankee and Doodle followed the wagon ahead of them.

"Hi!" she heard a small voice call.

She looked down. Beside her wagon skipped the pretty little blond girl who'd charmed everyone at their get-acquainted breakfast.

"Hi," said Stevie. "You're Eileen, aren't you?"

"Yes." Eileen smiled. She held up a straw basket filled

with angel-shaped cookies. "My mother baked these cookies and we were wondering if you'd like one."

"Sure," said Stevie. She reached down and grabbed a cookie from the basket. "Thanks."

"It's neat that you can drive a wagon and eat at the same time," Eileen said admiringly.

"Oh, it's not too hard," Stevie replied, her mouth full. "Would you like to learn how to drive?"

"Sure." Eileen's eyes were bright.

"Then climb up here and I'll show you." Stevie reached down to help her onto the wagon. In a moment Eileen was sitting beside her.

"Okay, Eileen. Here's what you do. Put the left rein over the index finger of your left hand, then put the right rein under your middle finger." Stevie helped Eileen arrange the reins in her hand. "Then hold your hand right at your belly button with your knuckles facing the horses."

Eileen positioned her hand as Stevie had showed her. "Is that all?" She looked up at Stevie with pale green eyes.

"Just about," said Stevie.

Eileen frowned as Yankee and Doodle trudged along. "How could you make them go faster?"

"Oh, you just pop a whip over their heads, or you pop the reins, if you haven't got a whip."

"Like this?" Eileen took the long ends of the reins

63

and gave both horses a sudden, vicious swat on their rumps.

"No!" Stevie cried, but it was too late. Yankee whinnied and reared in the traces, and then both horses surged forward at a gallop.

The jolt somersaulted Eileen backward into the wagon and loosened the reins in her hand. Stevie had just enough time to grab them before they fell between the horses' thundering feet. Quickly she grasped them in her left hand and braced herself against the footboard of the wagon. "Whoa!" she called, pulling hard on the reins. "Whoa!"

The horses did not stop. They galloped straight for the wagon in front of them, where a little boy sat in the back, a look of terror on his face. Stevie realized she would have to turn the team quickly if she was to avoid a real disaster.

"Haw!" she cried as loudly as she could, using both hands to turn the horses to the left. "Haw, Yankee! Haw, Doodle!"

The horses drew closer. Just as they were about to lunge into the wagon, Doodle pulled to the left. Yankee followed. Stevie's wagon flew past the other wagon in a blur, stirring up a huge cloud of yellow dust.

"Hey!" Stevie heard an angry voice shout over the sound of other horses whinnying. "No racing! You're messing up the order of the train!"

"I'm not racing!" Stevie said through gritted teeth as she pulled back on the reins with all her strength. "I'm trying to stop!"

Finally Yankee and Doodle slowed to a trot, and Stevie managed to pull them to a stop just as they drew up even with the lead wagon. For a moment it was all she could do just to breathe through the thick dust.

"Everything okay here?" Jeremy galloped up on his paint, frowning.

"Fine, now," gasped Stevie, red-faced and still out of breath.

"Well, take your place back in line when you can," he said firmly as he turned back to the head of the column.

"Just a minute." Stevie heard a small voice behind her. Eileen scrambled out from inside the wagon and climbed to the ground. "Some driving teacher you are," she said, glaring up at Stevie. "Look what you did to my angel cookies!" She held up the basket of broken cookies for Stevie to see.

"Well, gosh, so sorry," Stevie muttered. She started to add that she and Eileen could have wound up as crumbled as the cookies, but Eileen was already running back to the other wagons. Stevie shook her head and pulled Yankee and Doodle around, waiting to take her place in the line. As she waited, she watched Eileen run up and down the wagon train, showing everybody her broken cookies and pointing at Stevie.

"Some little angel you turned out to be," Stevie whispered. "From now on it'll just be heavenly if you stay away from me."

WHEN THE THICK yellow dust finally settled, Stevie saw her old place in the line and maneuvered the horses back into it. The little boy still looked out the back of the wagon she followed, only now he shook his finger at Stevie, as if she'd done something very bad.

Stevie wanted to make a face at the kid, but instead she gave him a sweet smile and kept Yankee and Doodle at a safe distance. There was no point in acting like a jerk to a little kid who didn't realize what had really happened. She took a deep breath and was trying to relax back into the bumpy rhythm of the wagon when she saw Gabriel riding toward her. He sat easily in the saddle as his bay horse loped along, and he wore his cowboy hat tilted forward on his head.

"You need to keep these horses in line," he said, reining up beside her. "We ride this way for a reason. And green drivers like you shouldn't be trying to race. It makes the other horses nervous and scares everybody on the wagons."

"Green drivers?" Stevie squawked, barely believing her ears. This arrogant tinhorn thought she was green!

"Yeah. Green drivers. No experienced driver would have done what you did. You can harness horses up okay, but I don't think you know a thing about driving them." He gave her a tight smile. "Just keep in line and follow the wagon in front of you. Do that and you'll be fine."

Stevie glared at him. She wanted to explain what had really happened, but she was so angry she could barely speak. "Well, thanks for your advice, Mr. Assistant Trail Boss," she finally managed to say. "I never would have figured it out all by myself."

"Just trying to help a lady." Smugly Gabriel tipped his hat and turned his horse back to the front of the line.

Stevie was so furious she thought she might explode. *What an idiot!* she fumed silently as she watched him ride away. *He's as bad as the kid in the next wagon. They both think they know exactly what happened when they know nothing at all!*

After Stevie had counted to ten several times, she calmed down enough to enjoy the rest of the afternoon. Yankee and Doodle pulled the wagon steadily, and as the sun began to set behind the far hills, Jeremy waved his hat around his head, the signal for everyone to circle up for the night. Stevie pulled into place and the girls began to work at making their camp. Stevie unhitched the team, fed them, and turned them out in the makeshift corral. Lisa watered Veronica and hitched her to the wagon wheel while Carole unsaddled Nikkia and gave him a good brushing. When they had finished taking care of their livestock, they wearily washed the gritty dust from their faces in a small creek and decided it might be a good night to sleep under the stars.

"I understand now why the pioneers turned in early," said Carole as she pulled her sleeping bag out of the wagon.

"Why?" asked Lisa.

"Because look at all this work we've done just to get ready to go to bed, and we still have to help with supper."

"I know," said Stevie, grabbing her own sleeping bag

and wincing from the blisters on her fingers. "I sure do miss Deborah. She would have been an extra pair of hands."

After the girls had joined some other campers in helping Shelly Bean with dinner, they took their seats around the campfire. Mr. Cate played his harmonica while Jeremy sat on a log, telling more history of the Oregon Trail.

"In the early 1800s, Lewis and Clark, helped by the Shoshone woman Sacagawea, charted the trail to the Northwest. After that, there was a big dispute over whether the land there really belonged to England or the United States. In 1841 the first group of settlers left the banks of the Missouri River and headed west toward the promised land of Oregon." Jeremy gazed into the crackling fire. "Those pioneers pushed the western boundary of America to the Pacific Ocean, and Oregon joined the union in 1859."

The girls' eyes glowed with admiration at what these brave pioneers had accomplished so many years before, and they listened carefully as Jeremy spoke of some of the more famous settlers who might have camped in that very spot. Finally, as the embers of the fire began to die, Lisa yawned and stood up.

"I don't know about you guys, but I'm beat," she said. "My shoulders hurt from tugging Veronica, my feet hurt from walking, and my legs hurt from doing everything else. I'm going to bed."

"Me too," said Carole, joining her in a yawn. "All the same parts of me ache as well. How about you, Stevie?"

"Count me in." Stevie got up slowly. "And ditto on the body parts. I sure wish we had a big feather bed to sleep in."

The girls walked over to their wagon. They had just arranged their sleeping bags on a soft bit of ground when Jeremy walked up.

"Hi, girls." He took off his cowboy hat. "I wanted to let you know that I just got a call from Deborah on my cell phone. She got back to Virginia safely and she's with her parents. Her dad's got a few broken bones and he's real sore, but he's going to be fine. And her mother's much calmer now that Deborah's there."

"That's wonderful news," said Carole.

Jeremy nodded. "She said to tell you three to be brave pioneers."

"Hey, speaking of being brave pioneers," Stevie said suddenly, "I'd like to explain what happened today, Jeremy. I wasn't trying to race with the other wagons. I was just showing that little girl Eileen how to hold the reins when she slapped both horses on their rumps. Yankee reared and bolted, and Doodle took off right along with him. I'm sorry if I scared the other people on the wagon train."

Jeremy's eyes grew serious. "Stevie, you don't need to apologize. I saw the whole thing. You were trying to be nice to Eileen, and you simply misjudged her capacity for misbehavior. I thought you did a fine job of getting your team back under control. You're probably one of the few people on this trip who could have done that."

Stevie began to blush. "Thanks."

Jeremy smiled and put his hat back on. "Well, you girls get a good night's sleep. You know how early five-thirty comes."

"Good night, Jeremy," they called as he walked over to his own camp.

The girls climbed into their sleeping bags. Above them, filmy clouds floated across the moon, and the sounds of Mr. Cate's harmonica floated over the camp-site. Stevie lit her tiny oil lamp and pulled her journal from beneath her pillow.

"Stevie, are you writing again tonight?" Carole yawned.

"Just for a few minutes," replied Stevie. She read over what she'd written the night before, then turned to a fresh page. *Day Two*, she wrote at the top.

Today was very exciting. Yankee and Doodle ran away with the wagon. Though it was really scary, I got

72

them back under control. Then Mr. Know-It-All Gabriel rode up and told me that I was a green driver who didn't know anything. I was furious! He is the most arrogant, obnoxious person I've ever met. But when he told me how I really didn't know what I was doing, his eyes turned this deep shade of blue, and when he rode away, he sat on the horse like his legs had been made for the saddle. And he wears his cowboy hat this really neat way that makes him look so cool.

"Wait a minute." Stevie blinked, rereading the words she'd just written. "This isn't what I wanted to say at all." She stared at the writing and wondered if she should cross it out or just start all over on a fresh page. Finally she tore the page out of the book and wadded it into a ball. *I'll toss that one into the campfire tomorrow morning,* she thought as she rolled over to sleep. *And maybe overnight I'll think of what I really want to say.*

From her own sleeping bag, Lisa heard Stevie rip the page from her book and then turn over to go to sleep. She smiled. *Stevie must be having a hard time driving a wagon all day and writing about it at night.* Lisa didn't blame her. She felt as if she was having a hard time doing everything from keeping up with Veronica to washing her face in the cold, muddy creeks. She sighed. How wonderful it would be to jump into a steaming hot shower and then into a soft, cozy bed. *You must be more like your mother than you thought,* a little voice whispered to her just as she was falling asleep. *All these modern comforts are as important to you as they are to her.*

No, they're not, Lisa protested sleepily. *Showers and beds and indoor toilets aren't important at all when you can look at the stars at night and smell the breeze that blows over the plains and listen to meadowlarks singing in the trees.* The little voice kept whispering, though, until Lisa finally rolled over in her sleeping bag and pulled the blankets to her chin. Just as she felt herself falling into a deep and restful sleep, something cold and wet splashed on her cheek. She opened her eyes. Another wet something hit her, then another after that. She sat up. A gentle but insistent rain had begun to fall.

"Stevie! Carole! Wake up!" Lisa shook her friends. "It's raining. We need to get under some shelter."

Fumbling in the dark, the girls got up, pulled their sleeping bags beneath the wagon, and settled down again to sleep. The ground was a lot harder under the wagon, and what felt like a dozen small rocks dug into Lisa's back. *Be brave,* she told herself, twisting and turning as she tried to get comfortable. *The pioneers had to cope with rain and pain and tiredness, and you can, too.*

"Is anybody awake but me?" Lisa rose up on one elbow and peered through the dim light.

"I am," muttered Carole. "I woke up when that darn prairie chicken started chirping."

"I'm not." Stevie's voice was muffled by her sleeping bag. "I'm having a nightmare that I'm awake. I'm actually still sound asleep."

Lisa ran one hand through her short, sun-streaked hair. "I don't know about you guys, but I don't think I slept a wink all night. It felt like a small river was flowing underneath me."

Stevie sat up and felt the underside of her sleeping

bag. "I think we must have slept downhill from some runoff," she said. "My sleeping bag is soggy."

"Let's get dressed," said Carole. "That way at least our outside clothes will help get us warm and dry."

Lisa watched as Stevie and Carole scrambled out from under the wagon; then she followed them. The night before, her arms had ached from tugging Veronica along. Now her back was sore from having slept on the rocky ground. As she slowly pulled her sleeping bag from beneath the wagon, she wished, for an instant, that this wagon train reenactment was over and that she was back in civilization, sleeping in a soft bed in warm, dry pajamas.

You really are like your mother, the little voice chirped inside her head.

No, I'm not, she argued silently. *I left all those spoiled ideas back in Virginia, just like I left my suitcases stashed in Stevie's closet.*

I don't think so, said the singsong voice. *Yes, I did*, Lisa insisted, refusing to listen anymore. She threw her sleeping bag into the wagon and climbed up after it. She was determined not to complain about anything that day, especially things as silly as wet clothes and a sore back.

"Yuck," Stevie said as she pulled her dress on over her head. "This scratchy old dress feels awful against my skin."

"I know." Carole buttoned her blue shirt. "And this wagon is so dark you can barely see what you're putting on." She zipped her jeans. "I don't guess that matters, though, since we only have one outfit to wear."

"Oh, it's not so bad." Lisa tried her best to sound cheerful. "I mean, the pioneers had to dress in here, and their wagons were a lot more crowded with stuff than ours is." She held up her blue dress and noticed that the hem was covered with mud and that dust had settled in the fringes around the collar. "After all, we're here to get a taste of what pioneer life was like. They didn't have umbrellas and hair dryers and microwaves. All they had was what they could carry, and they couldn't carry much in these little wagons."

"Right now I wish this one was carrying a nice hot shower," said Stevie.

"Maybe if we don't complain it won't seem so bad." Lisa pulled her dress on. "You know, keep a stiff upper lip and everything. After all, we've got a job to do." She sat down and began to put on her shoes. "In fact, we've got several jobs to do. We've got to learn all about the trip and the land, and do our research for Deborah's article, and take care of our animals, plus all the other basic stuff, like surviving."

"And like not letting Gabriel get under our skin." Stevie pushed up the sleeves of her dress and frowned. "He is such a creep."

77

"He is pretty arrogant," Carole agreed, tying her long hair in a ponytail.

"Watch out, then." Lisa looked out the back of the wagon. "Here comes Mr. Arrogant Creep now."

Gabriel sauntered up to the back of their wagon. "Hi," he said, smiling his funny, lopsided smile. "How are you ladies doing this morning?"

"Fine," snapped Stevie, her hazel eyes flashing.

"Well," he said, laughing, "you're the only girls on this trip who are. Every other female I've talked to this morning has only complained about the weather. 'It was soooo nasty last night,'" he mimicked in a high voice. "'All my clothes got wet and my hair's a mess! I miss my hair dryer!'" Gabriel gave a snort. "I think this trip might be too tough for girls, if all they can do is whine about one night of light rain!"

Carole and Lisa felt Stevie twitch between them. They knew how infuriating Gabriel's words were to her. Lisa quickly shifted in front of her while Carole grabbed the back of her dress. It would do no good for Stevie to pounce on Gabriel like a mountain lion in front of the whole camp!

Gabriel continued, obviously unaware that he had insulted The Saddle Club and every other female on the trip. "Anyway, I won't have to put up with any slackers today. As assistant trail boss, I get to ride with

78

one of the scouts to make sure the trail ahead is clear."
He smiled at the girls and tipped his hat. "So I hope
you ladies have a nice, dry, comfy day!"

"It's looking sunnier already," Stevie called as Gabriel strolled over toward Jeremy's camp.

When he was out of sight, the girls turned back inside their wagon.

"Can you believe him?" Stevie clenched her fists in
frustration.

"No." Carole shook her head. "Actually, I can't."

"Boy, I can think of about a hundred jokes I'd like to
play on him. Starting with greasing his saddle so that he
can't stay on his horse and then gluing the inside of his
stupid old hat so that he can't tip it to the 'ladies'
anymore!"

"Stevie!" Lisa warned. "You could get into some serious trouble if you started playing your practical jokes
here."

"I know," Stevie replied, realizing that she had to
behave. "Getting into trouble would be bad; Deborah is
counting on us." She sighed; then she looked at Carole
and Lisa and smiled. "Anyway, there are so many wonderful things going on here, how could I possibly be
thinking about getting into trouble?"

"Wonderful things?" Lisa raised one eyebrow. "Like
what?"

Stevie grinned. "Like we're here in the middle of this beautiful country reenacting this wonderful piece of history!"

"Well, yes," Lisa agreed. "And apparently we're the only females on this wagon train who aren't complaining about it."

"Right!" said Stevie. "See how much better things are already? And we won't have to deal with that jerk Gabriel for the rest of the day! He'll be out of our hair until the campfire tonight, and that's the most wonderful thing imaginable!"

The girls hopped out of the wagon to find that the day was sunny and bright. The night's rain had washed the mugginess out of the air, and everything sparkled as if it were brand new. They ate their mush for breakfast, then broke camp with everyone else. Stevie hitched up Yankee and Doodle more smoothly than she ever had before, and Carole found Nikkia's trot a lot easier to sit. And though Lisa was sore from her night underneath the wagon, Veronica seemed well rested and had caught on to the fact that she was supposed to walk with them instead of wandering around the plains munching grass.

The Saddle Club moved up one place in line and headed west. With Gabriel scouting ahead of them and bratty Eileen remaining with her own family, they had a good morning. Stevie and Lisa switched jobs once,

80

and Lisa was about to trade off driving with Carole when Jeremy halted the train for lunch.

"Thank goodness!" said Lisa as she pulled Yankee and Doodle to a stop. "I was just hoping we would break for lunch."

Carole glanced over at her friend and noticed dark circles underneath her eyes. "Lisa, you're looking a little tired," she said. "Why don't you take a nap after lunch? Stevie and I can handle your share of the chores, and I'll volunteer to milk Veronica for anybody who would like some fresh milk."

Lisa's mouth fell open. "Where did you learn to milk a cow?"

"Oh, it's part of Marine Corps basic training," Carole replied, then burst out laughing at Lisa's astonished expression. "Actually, I learned on my aunt's farm in Minnesota. They have a holstein named Cora Mae."

Lisa smiled in gratitude. "Carole, that would be wonderful. I could use a little extra sleep."

"And I bet some of these pioneers could use a glass of milk!"

After lunch Stevie helped clean up while Lisa retreated to the wagon for a nap. Though Carole's own arms and legs ached from riding and driving, she tied Veronica to one of the few trees growing nearby and sat down on a milking stool beside her. A small crowd of pioneers gathered around to watch.

"Okay, Veronica," Carole said to the cow, which turned and gave her a dubious look. "Let's show these people what you can do."

Hoping that she hadn't forgotten all the milking skills she'd learned in Minnesota, Carole placed a bucket beneath the cow and gave one of her udders a pull and a squeeze. Veronica shifted once on her feet; then suddenly a stream of white milk began to clatter into the bucket. A cheer went up from the crowd.

"Wow, Carole," said Polly Shaver. "That's neat."

"Yeah," a man agreed. "We didn't think you could really do it."

Carole smiled. "Actually, Veronica's the one doing most of it. I'm just sort of at the right place at the right time."

"Can I have a taste?" a little boy asked.

"Sure," said Carole. "Let me get this bucket a little fuller."

Veronica gave a half bucket of milk. Everybody who wanted some got some.

Awhile later Lisa climbed out of the wagon, looking rested and refreshed. "Did Veronica do okay?" she asked, looking at the cow, which had again wandered off to browse in the grass.

"She was the hit of the day." Carole grinned.

"Thanks for helping me out like that, Carole," said Lisa. "I feel so much better."

"Well, that's what The Saddle Club is all about," said Carole.

"Maybe that's what the pioneer spirit is all about, too," said Stevie, who had just finished the milk she'd scooped from Carole's bucket. "Anyway, now we need to get going. The train's rolling west."

They resumed their old jobs, but this time with lighter hearts. Though they still had their various aches and pains, they rode along thinking that problems didn't seem nearly as bad when you were with people who shared them right along with you, and who were happy to help you whenever they could.

THAT EVENING A crimson sunset blazed in the western sky. Stevie and Carole and Lisa sat enjoying it beside the campfire as they finished the last of their supper. Just as the sun finally slipped behind the distant mountains, Mr. Cate began to play a soft tune on his harmonica and Jeremy stood up to start their nightly campfire session.

"Tonight, instead of talking about the history of the Oregon Trail, we're going to do something a little different," he announced with a devilish gleam in his eye. "We're going to do what the pioneers often did after a long, hard day on the trail."

"What's that?" someone asked from across the fire.

Jeremy grinned. "We're going to entertain each other with stories. Tall tales, jokes, riddles, anything you want. It's all up to you."

Stevie winked at Lisa and Carole as she raised her hand. "Hey, Jeremy, can we tell ghost stories?"

"We sure can," he replied. "Are you volunteering to tell the first one?"

"Why, yes," Stevie said. "As a matter of fact, I am."

"Then stand up here by the fire so that everyone can hear you, and scare us to death." Jeremy led the campers in a round of applause as Stevie approached the fire. "Ladies and gentlemen, the best ghost-story teller in Virginia, Ms. Stevie Lake."

Stevie bowed deeply and began her story. Though Lisa and Carole had heard it many times before—the legend of a ghost stallion that seeks revenge on the drovers who rounded up his herd—that night Stevie changed the setting from Virginia to the Western plains and transformed the Chincoteague Island ponies to wild mustangs. Everyone's eyes grew wide as Stevie described the terror of the drovers who kept hearing ghostly hoofbeats bearing down upon them when there was nothing there. Finally, just as Stevie reached the climax of her story, one of the real wagon train horses let out a single shrill scream. Everybody nearly jumped out of their skin.

"And the stallion lives on to this day," Stevie finished with a flourish, "still searching for anyone who has ever hurt a horse. That might even be him right now, looking for you!"

Except for two people, everyone burst into applause. To Stevie's delight, little Eileen sat trembling in her mother's lap, her arms clutching her mother's neck in terror. Gabriel, on the other hand, had pushed his cowboy hat back on his head and was giving Stevie a curious, unreadable look.

"Thank you, Stevie," said Jeremy. "That was great. Anybody else have an entertainment for the evening?"

"I do," Gabriel announced.

"Let's have it, then," said Jeremy.

Stevie sat down, shrugging at Carole and Lisa as Gabriel sauntered to the middle of the circle.

"Does everyone realize this is Crow country?" Gabriel began. He stood in the circle and began talking about an Indian brave who'd killed his blood brother. He hadn't spoken a minute before Stevie realized that this was a ghost story, too. Gabriel was trying to one-up her! Not only did he think he knew everything about horses and wagons and the Oregon Trail, he thought he was the best ghost-story teller on the planet as well. *No way*, Stevie silently vowed as Gabriel spoke in eerie tones over the fire. *I'm a hundred times better than he is, and I'll prove it if I have to tell ghost stories all night.*

Gabriel ended his tale with a war whoop, which again made everyone jump and made little Eileen cover her ears.

"Anybody else?" Jeremy asked after Gabriel sat down.

"I've got another," Stevie called out, giving Gabriel a steely glare. "And it's the scariest story in the world!"

"Go, Stevie!" another camper called. "We want some more of yours!"

"Okay, Stevie, you're on again." Jeremy laughed and sat down. Everyone's eyes turned to Stevie.

"Once upon a time," she began, standing close to the fire so that the flames would make her cheeks and chin look scary, "there was a young man who feared rats more than anything in the world. . . ."

A hush fell on the campers as Stevie wove her tale of murder and revenge. Little Eileen began to cry, and as Stevie's voice rose in conclusion, all the campers gazed at her in rapt attention.

"And every time you hear scratching that you can't explain, just remember that man and what the rats did to him!"

Everybody murmured approval when the story was over, and Stevie sat down to great applause.

"Wow, Stevie, I've heard you tell that one before, but never that well." Carole rubbed her arms and shivered. "You really gave me the chills."

"Yeah, Stevie, that was great!" Lisa said with a smile.

Gabriel was halfway back to the campfire when Jeremy stopped him. "I'm afraid that's all we have time for tonight. We've got a big day tomorrow. We're going to be crossing the river, plus tomorrow night the dude ranchers are going to be joining us. I think right now all of us had better call it a day and get a good night's sleep."

The campers stretched their legs and got up slowly, yawning as they made their way to their sleeping bags. Several people congratulated Stevie on her storytelling as they went to their own campsites.

"Where shall we sleep tonight?" asked Carole when the girls reached their wagon. "Inside, outside, or underneath the wagon?"

Lisa looked up at the twinkling stars. "Oh, let's sleep outside. The ground is softer than the wagon floor, and there's not a cloud in the sky. It couldn't possibly rain again."

They pulled their sleeping bags to a grassy little dip in the ground and settled in. After Lisa and Carole had said good night, Stevie lit the oil lamp and reached for her journal. Her body was tired, but her mind was still wide awake from all the fun she'd had.

Day Three

Today was the best day yet. After a rainy, sleepless night, we woke up to beautiful weather. All our work went a lot easier, and we traded off jobs several times during the afternoon. After lunch Carole milked the cow and gave everyone fresh milk. At the campfire tonight I told two of my favorite ghost stories. The last one scared that little creep Eileen so much she began to cry, but I don't care. After her stunt with the horses, it's exactly what she deserves. Most of the people on this trip are really nice, and the campfire tonight was the most fun yet.

She read over her words and smiled. This journal had been a great idea. She could read these pages when she was eighty and remember what a wonderful time she'd had. She stuffed the little book under her pillow and blew out the lamp, but instead of rolling over to sleep, she folded her arms beneath her head and stared up into the sky. A fragrant breeze was blowing from the southwest, and overhead a billion stars twinkled in the heavens. She sighed and thought of Phil. *Somewhere, perhaps a thousand miles away, he's probably lying in a sleeping bag near a river, tired from a day of rafting and fun, just like I'm tired from a day of wagon training and fun. Even when we're far away from one another, we're doing exactly the same thing at the same time.* Sighing happily, she started to gaze at one star that had a reddish twinkle and remembered what Carole had said about absence making the heart grow fonder. She pictured Phil's warm smile; then suddenly Gabriel's face flashed before her. She frowned. That wasn't supposed to happen! Suddenly she heard a whisper.

"Stevie? Why are you still awake?"

Stevie turned and looked at Lisa. "I don't know. I just am."

"What are you thinking about?"

"Yeah, Stevie," Carole chimed in. "I could tell you weren't asleep, too." She sat up in her sleeping bag.

Stevie raised herself on one elbow. "Actually, I was thinking about Phil. About how neat it is that he and I are probably a thousand miles apart but we're still doing exactly the same thing. You know, sleeping under the stars and everything."

"That is neat," agreed Lisa.

Then Stevie sighed again and idly snapped a button on her sleeping bag. "But I was also thinking about Gabriel."

"Gabriel?" Lisa asked in disbelief.

Stevie nodded. "You know how annoying he is—how

he puts on that Mr. Superior attitude and struts around here like some movie cowboy."

"Yes?"

"Well, there's something else, too. I mean, have you ever noticed how blue his eyes get when he's being such a jerk? And how when he's acting his worst he grins the most mischievous grin in the world? And have you seen the way he wears his hat?"

"Stevie!" Lisa cried. "You've got a crush on him!"

"Shhh!" Stevie hissed. "Don't talk so loud! The whole camp's going to hear you! And besides, I don't have a crush on him. I just think he's kind of interesting, in a way. Don't you think so?"

"Sure," said Carole. "He's fascinating if you like an obnoxious jerk who thinks he knows everything and doesn't mind telling you about it."

"And if you like someone who assumes you're the dumbest person in the world before you've even said a word," Lisa added.

"Oh, I don't think he's that bad." Stevie turned and vigorously fluffed her pillow.

Lisa shook her head. "Look. If we're sitting here in the middle of the night having a conversation about whether or not Gabriel is cute, then we definitely didn't get enough sleep last night! We're so tired, we're probably not thinking straight, and five-thirty in the morning is going to be here in about five minutes."

91

"She's right." Carole flopped back down in her sleeping bag. "I'm going to sleep. Stevie, you'll have to figure out Gabriel's cuteness quotient all by yourself."

"Okay, okay," Stevie said as her friends rolled over and went to sleep. She snuggled down in her own sleeping bag and closed her eyes, but her mind spun with thoughts of Phil and Gabriel. *Okay,* she told herself, *so you find that a basically obnoxious boy has some attractive features. So what? It doesn't mean you have some big-deal crush on him. You just realize that jerks can have nice qualities, too.* She looked over at Carole and Lisa. *You certainly don't have to make excuses to your friends for that. But*—she frowned as she looked at Carole—*didn't Carole say that absence would make my heart grow fonder? If my heart's growing fonder of Phil, then why are my eyes suddenly starting to wander? And what if Phil's eyes are wandering just like mine? What if a thousand miles away there's some cute Ms. Know-It-All on his rafting trip? Or maybe she isn't Ms. Know-It-All. Maybe she's Ms. Cuter-and-Smarter-Than-Me. Maybe she's even a better rider!* Stevie sat up straight in her sleeping bag, her heart thudding. *What if Phil's a thousand miles away falling in love with someone else?*

For a long time she stared at the dim orange glow of the banked campfire, almost wishing she'd canceled this trip and gone rafting with Phil and his family. Then at least if their hearts hadn't grown fonder, their eyes could only have wandered toward each other. Now there was probably some other wonderful, fabulous girl Phil had fallen for. *Oh, well.* She sighed as she once again flopped down in her sleeping bag. There was nothing she could do about Phil and his gorgeous new girlfriend that night. That night the only thing she could do was sleep, and that didn't sound like a half-bad idea.

IT SEEMED AS IF Stevie had just closed her eyes when the clang of the triangle jarred her awake. For a moment she lay in her sleeping bag, watching as Lisa and Carole scurried around getting dressed and brushing their teeth in a small wooden bucket of water.

"Come on, Stevie," Lisa said. "Get up. You're going to be late for breakfast."

Stevie rubbed her eyes. "You two go on over to the chuck wagon and save me a place in the chow line."

"Are you feeling okay?" asked Carole, knowing that Stevie was seldom late for a meal.

Stevie nodded. "I'll catch up to you in a minute."

Lisa and Carole walked over to breakfast while

Stevie rose slowly from her sleeping bag. She climbed into the wagon and found her tattered, scratchy dress. *Phil's new girlfriend probably wears really cool rafting outfits*, she thought glumly, changing from her T-shirt and shorts into the dress. *At least he's not here to see me in this getup*.

After she brushed her hair, she made her way over to the chow line. Lisa and Carole were about to be served. Stevie hurried and slipped in line behind Carole.

"Stevie, why are you such a storm cloud this morning?" Carole asked.

"I didn't sleep too well last night," Stevie muttered as she picked up a tin plate and spoon.

"Look what Mr. Assistant Trail Boss is doing this morning," Lisa whispered with a grin.

Stevie looked up at the steaming iron kettle at the head of the line. Gabriel stood there, helping Shelly spoon cornmeal mush onto everyone's plate.

Maybe I'll skip breakfast, Stevie thought as the line inched forward. Just as she was about to excuse herself, Gabriel saw her and grinned.

"Well, here's the ghost-story queen of Virginia and all her pals," he said as he slapped a serving of mush onto Lisa's plate. "I want to remind you ladies that it's probably not a good day to do any more wagon racing. We're going to be crossing the river, and that can be dangerous."

95

"No kidding," Stevie said with a smirk.

Gabriel slapped some mush onto her plate. "So you need to be extra careful and pay attention to what the trail bosses tell you to do."

Stevie had opened her mouth to reply when Carole grabbed her arm. "Come on, Stevie. Let's have a nice, peaceful breakfast over there by the tree."

Lisa and Carole hurried Stevie over to a single small pine tree. "You know," Carole said as she sat down beneath the scraggly tree, "I think he must be the biggest jerk I've ever met."

Stevie sat down. Amazingly, she suddenly felt wonderful. As she listened to Carole it occurred to her that she couldn't possibly be interested in someone that painfully obnoxious. She might appreciate some things about him, but like him? Forget it! And that meant that Phil couldn't possibly be interested in the girl he'd just met. Oh, he might like her eyes and her laugh and her cute outfits, but that didn't mean he was going to do anything drastic, like fall in love with her!

Stevie started beaming. "You know," she said to her puzzled friends, "this might turn out to be the best day yet!"

After breakfast Jeremy called a brief camp meeting. "I want to explain a little bit about river crossings," he said, taking off his hat in the bright sunlight. "This river we're crossing today can be dangerous, but we're going over at its widest, shallowest point. We haven't had a lot of rain, so the water should be at a manageable level. For those of you riding horses or tending livestock, the best way to cross is to simply ride or lead your horse or cow into the water. Most animals are natural swimmers and won't have any problem. Don't try to pull them along or make them go any faster than they want to. And of course, if your animal gets into trouble, let it go and get to shore yourself. Animals know how to take care of themselves."

Jeremy looked at Stevie. "For you wagoneers, just drive your team into the river. The horses will swim, and your wagon will float. It also may leak a little, so the trick is to get across as fast as you safely can. That way your supplies won't get too wet. Again, if your wagon should get into trouble, leave it and get to shore yourself."

Jeremy looked at the suddenly grim faces of the campers and smiled. "Let me assure you that I've led wagon trains across this river for fifteen years, and the worst thing I've ever lost was someone's watch." He brushed his gray hair back and resettled his hat. "Okay, pioneers, let's get rolling."

"Are you guys scared?" Carole asked Lisa and Stevie when they were ready to go.

"A little," admitted Stevie. "Although I sure wasn't going to let Jeremy know."

"I just hope Veronica can swim faster than she walks," said Lisa, looking at the placid cow. "Otherwise, she and I might float on down to the Gulf of Mexico."

Suddenly Jeremy's sharp "Wagons ho!" pierced the bright air.

"Good luck, guys," said Stevie, clucking to the horses. "Here we go."

The wagons rolled westward. Slowly the flat land they had been traveling over became hillier, and as they neared the river, gnarled trees climbed up its steep banks. A large flock of yellow-headed blackbirds nested in the trees, cawing in alarm as the wagon train grew near. Stevie maneuvered the wagon as close to the river as she could; then The Saddle Club watched as the wagon ahead of them began to make the crossing.

It crossed the blue water quickly. It floated a little off course in the middle of the stream, but nothing fell off, and the horses pulled it well up on the opposite bank.

"Next!" Jeremy called.

"Our turn," said Stevie. "Why don't you two go first? That other wagon didn't have livestock with it. You guys can get Nikkia and Veronica across, then come back and help me with Yankee and Doodle."

"Good idea," said Carole. She looked at Lisa. "Do you want to go first or shall I?"

"Better let me start," said Lisa. "It'll probably take Veronica three hours to wander across anyway."

"Good luck," Stevie and Carole called as Lisa led Veronica down to the river.

"See you in Acapulco," Lisa laughed.

Lisa stopped on the riverbank. The water, which had looked like a lazy stream from where they had watched the first wagon cross, now seemed more like a rushing torrent. She wondered how deep it was in the middle, then decided it didn't matter. She was on this trip and she was a pioneer. Somehow she would have to get this cow across this river. "Ready, Veronica?" she asked. Veronica looked at the river and continued chewing her cud.

"Well, I'll take that as a big yes," Lisa said. She grasped the lead rope tightly, took a deep breath, and waded into the cold water. She fully expected to feel a tug on the rope, which would mean that Veronica had planted herself firmly on the shore, but to her surprise, Veronica's head began bobbing along right beside her. "Way to go, Veronica!" Lisa said, stunned at the cow's strong, even strokes. "You're a regular mermaid!" Veronica's determined expression looked so comical that Lisa laughed, stepped in a hole, and wound up gulping a mouthful of river water. Suddenly she realized that Veronica was doing fine and she was the one who'd better pay more attention. After a few quick swimming strokes of her own, she pulled Veronica triumphantly to the other side of the river, sending Carole and Stevie a thumbs-up sign.

Next it was Carole's turn. "Come on, Nikkia," Carole said. "Time to go for a swim." The big Appaloosa looked at the water dubiously and backed up a step. Carole urged him forward. He took a sideways step toward the river and stopped. "Let's go, Nikkia," Carole repeated. The horse snorted and shook his head. "Okay. Don't say I didn't warn you," Carole said firmly. She shifted her weight forward in the saddle and gave the horse a loud pop on his rump. Surprised, Nikkia bounded into the river. For a moment Carole thought he might rear, but he found his swimming stride quickly and in a little while they were both shaking water off on the other bank.

"Let's go back and get Stevie now," Lisa said, holding Nikkia's bridle while Carole dismounted from the dripping horse. They tethered Nikkia and Veronica to a nearby tree and then swam back across the river to Stevie.

"Yankee and Doodle seem pretty calm," said Stevie as Lisa and Carole waded out of the river. "I think they've done this before."

"That's a relief," said Carole.

Lisa grabbed Yankee's halter while Carole took hold

of Doodle's, and slowly they led the horses into the river. At first the wagon just creaked along the sandy bottom, but then, as the river deepened, the current lifted and buoyed the wagon. "We're floating!" Stevie called. "We're now officially a boat!"

They reached the other side of the river quickly. The horses shook the water from their coats. Lisa and Carole let go of their halters and Stevie drove them close to where Nikkia and Veronica were tied. "Good boys!" She rubbed them both as she tied them to a tree. "I'm going to sneak you two an apple after lunch!" Suddenly she turned. Someone down by the river was screaming.

She ran back down to the bank. Midway across the river, a wagon had turned over. Though the horses and passengers were safe, all the wagon's supplies were drifting downstream. People on the bank were yelling at Carole and Lisa, who were already swimming out to rescue everything they could grab.

"Wait for me!" cried Stevie, tearing off her boots and hurrying to the shore. She waded into the water and started swimming just as someone else plunged into the river behind her.

Carole and Lisa had spread out in the water. "You grab those bedrolls," Carole called to Lisa. "I'll try to get this backpack."

"What should I get?" asked Stevie, paddling frantically.

101

"Anything else you can," called Lisa.

A cell phone floated by Stevie's ear. She grabbed it and looked around for something else that might be drifting away, but instead of seeing spilled supplies, she saw Gabriel behind her, grappling with a huge, over-stuffed suitcase.

"Here," she said, swimming over to him. "Let me help."

"Lift one end up and it won't get so wet," he said, spitting out a mouthful of water.

Together they maneuvered the suitcase to the river-bank just as Lisa and Carole waded out with all the bedrolls and the backpack. A crowd of people gathered around as they came ashore.

"Oh, girls," a pretty blond woman said as they stood gasping for breath. "I can't thank you enough! You've saved all our important supplies!"

"And you girls did it just like the real pioneers!" Polly said.

"They didn't save my teddy bear!" shrieked a small voice behind Stevie. She knew without looking whose voice that was. It was little Eileen's.

Mr. Cate started to laugh at Eileen. "Why is a big girl like you crying about a teddy bear? Your parents could have lost everything they brought with them!"

"Because it was *my* teddy bear!" Eileen shrieked even

102

more loudly. "Mommy! They lost Teddy! They lost *my* Teddy!"

"Shhh, Eileen," said her mother, suddenly embarrassed. She leaned over and wrapped her arms around the weeping girl. "Let's sit over here on the bank with Daddy and calm down."

Suddenly Jeremy rushed up. "Is everyone okay?" he asked.

"Sure," said Gabriel. "We're fine."

"That was quite a rescue you put on. I was busy with their horses, but I saw most of it. The four of you certainly work well together as a team." Jeremy smiled.

"Actually, we did," replied Stevie, glaring at Gabriel. "Imagine that. Menfolk and womenfolk, working together."

Gabriel ignored her and looked at Jeremy, who was squinting at the wagons waiting on the far shore. "After the rest of the wagons cross the river, we'll be on our way," Jeremy said. "We won't go too much farther today, so you folks can take it easy. A river crossing kind of takes the starch out of everybody."

"You can say that again," laughed Lisa, wringing a stream of water out of her skirt.

By midafternoon the wagon train had stopped for the night. Stevie, Carole, and Lisa gave a sigh of relief as the wagons made their traditional circle, a formation the pioneers used to enclose their livestock more than to protect against Indians. As the girls pulled into position, their river-soaked clothes struck to their backs, and Lisa's wet socks squelched with every step she took.

"I vote we dress modern for a little while," she said as Stevie pushed the wagon's brake. "And try to get our pioneer clothes dry somehow."

"Sounds good to me," said Stevie.

They changed into their jeans and hung their wet clothes on some scrub pine that was growing near their wagon. Their normal clothes felt wonderfully comfortable, and for a long time they just relaxed on the ground, letting the afternoon sun warm their stiff muscles as it dried their dresses.

Suddenly Carole frowned. "Do you guys feel anything weird?"

"Weird like how?" Stevie asked.

"I don't know," said Carole. "It's like the ground is tingling."

"Tingling?" Stevie leaned over and put her hand flat on the sandy ground. "Good grief!" she cried. "It *is* tingling! Maybe we're sitting on some kind of underground volcano that's about to blow!"

"Hi, girls," Shelly Bean called, hurrying by. "Are you feeling the cattle yet?"

"The cattle?" Lisa asked.

"Yeah. The herd from the dude ranch. Just put your

hand to the ground and you can feel their hooves."
Shelly grinned and pointed over his shoulder. "You can
also see the dust they're raising on the horizon."

The girls looked where Shelly pointed. Sure enough,
a small cloud of brown dust was slowly drawing closer.

"So much for your underground volcano," Carole
laughed as Stevie's face turned red.

They watched as the dust cloud grew bigger. Finally
they could pick out individual riders moving a mass of
cows toward the river.

"Let's go over and say hello," Carole said, standing
on tiptoe as she watched the herd.

The girls joined some others in their group and
walked over to the dude ranch camp. An array of people much like their own greeted them—families, a couple of teenagers, and a few retired couples. They all
seemed comfortable on their cow ponies and eager to
share tales of their trip with the Oregon Trail folks.

"We hear you guys crossed the river today," a red-
headed young wrangler said.

"That's right," replied Stevie. "Some of us did it
more than once."

"Was it hard getting your wagons across?" a sun-
burned woman asked.

"Probably not as hard as two hundred cows," laughed
Carole.

A little boy in a white cowboy hat rode up on a fat

black pony. "Have you heard that we're going to have a big party tonight?"

"Yes," said Lisa. "And we're really looking forward to it."

"Our trail boss, Robbie, is going to play his fiddle and one of the cowboys is going to call a square dance!"

"That sounds like fun," said Stevie. She turned to Carole and Lisa. "Maybe we'd better go back to our camp and get into our outfits again."

"Good idea," Carole agreed. They said good-bye to their new cowboy friends and hurried back to their camp. Just when they had gotten their pioneer clothes back on, they heard the dinner triangle clanging loudly.

"Come and get it!" Shelly Bean had hopped up on a hay bale and was making a speech. "Tonight my buddy Sidewinder Slim and I have cooked y'all the most delicious, mouthwaterin', lip-smackin', hair-curlin' meal west of the Missouri! And anybody who ain't had two helpings before sundown is gonna hurt my feelings!"

"Whoa!" Carole laughed. "I guess we'd better go eat!"

They joined the others around a huge campfire. Shelly and Sidewinder Slim had truly come up with a feast, filling everybody's plates with thick steaks, piles of corn on the cob, and rhubarb-and-apple cobbler for dessert. Stevie, Lisa, and Carole ate until they couldn't eat anymore.

106

"Arrgggh," groaned Stevie. "I'm stuffed."

"You can't be stuffed now, Stevie," said Carole. "The dancing is about to begin."

Just as everybody finished supper, a cowboy from the dude ranch stood up by the campfire.

"Howdy, folks. My name's Rascal Robbie Robertson and I'm the head drover for this cattle drive. Tonight I'm going to prove that I can outfiddle anybody east of California and west of Nevada." He struck a chord on his fiddle. "And while I'm sawin' on this thing, my buddy Willowbark Bob here's gonna call some dances for you. So grab a partner and let's have some fun!"

Everybody cleared a large space in front of the fire. Rascal Robbie started to play, and soon six couples were dancing in a square to Willowbark Bob's calls.

A tall boy from the dude ranch came over and asked Lisa to dance, and then Stevie and Carole got up and danced with each other. As they did a ladies' chain around the square, Stevie noticed that Gabriel was dancing with one of the girls from the dude ranch. *Probably too chicken to dance with any of us*, she thought as she and Carole locked arms and swung each other in a wide circle.

Everyone danced until late in the evening. Only Eileen wasn't having fun. She complained to anyone who would listen that Stevie and Carole and Lisa and Gabriel had lost her teddy bear in the river on purpose.

Though everyone was sorry she'd lost her toy, nobody paid much attention to her accusations. Finally she gave up and wandered away by herself.

Later, when the fire had burned to embers, Rascal Robbie said it was time for his cowboys to go put their dogies to sleep, and the party broke up. The cowboys and the pioneers shook hands and wished each other good luck as they walked slowly back to their camps.

"Wasn't that the best time ever?" Lisa said as the girls pulled their sleeping bags out into the open air.

"It was great," said Carole. "And who was that boy you were dancing with? He was cute."

"He said his name was Ken," Lisa replied. "And he was cute, wasn't he? Too bad he's a cowboy and not a pioneer." She nestled down into her sleeping bag. "Are you writing again tonight, Stevie?" she asked.

"Yeah. Just a little." Stevie lit the oil lamp and wrote quickly.

Day Four
What a perfect day! We crossed the river, rescued some cargo, had a campfire and a hoedown. I wish Phil had been here—he would really have enjoyed it.

She read over her words once, blew out the lamp, and shoved the journal under her pillow. She was too tired to write anymore. She could fill in the details later.

Just as she closed her eyes to go to sleep, she heard an ugly howling sound. She lifted her head off the pillow and listened more closely, then shook her head and relaxed again. *Just the wind blowing through the scrub brush. Or maybe it's Gabriel,* she thought with a chuckle as she drifted off to sleep. *Trying to play some trick to prove he's scarier than me.*

CAROLE WOKE UP with a start. She'd been dreaming that a swarm of bees was chasing her and Starlight. They were getting closer and closer, and as fast as Starlight galloped, he couldn't outrun them.

Maybe I shouldn't have eaten so much cobbler, she thought as she rolled over in her sleeping bag. She fluffed her pillow and laid her head down. Oddly, she heard the same buzzing noise she'd just dreamed about. She lifted her head. The noise was gone. She laid her head back down. The noise was back.

"That's weird," she said aloud, sitting up. She put the palm of her hand down on the ground between her sleeping bag and Stevie's. The buzzing noise became more of a pounding. She felt the ground next to Lisa. It pounded even harder there. She blinked for a moment, and her heart skipped a beat. Suddenly she knew exactly what the noise was. The cattle were stampeding!

In a flash she was out of her sleeping bag. "Stevie! Lisa! Wake up! It's a stampede!"

"Uh?" said Stevie, blinking.

"The cattle are stampeding. And since they're down by the river, the only direction they can run is straight for our camp. We've got to stop them!"

Without another word, the girls scrambled into their jeans and boots. "What shall we do?" asked Lisa.

"We need to get to the corral and get on some horses, and wake up as many people as we can along the way."

"What if everyone panics?" Stevie's eyes were wide with alarm.

"We'll have to let Jeremy worry about that. If they get trampled by a herd of cattle, they'll be dead!"

The girls leaped out of their wagon and raced toward the corral. Carole and Stevie yelled, "Stampede! Everybody up!" while Lisa desperately looked for Jeremy. Most people just blinked at them sleepily, but a few understood what was going on. Karen Nicely wrapped a blanket around her shoulders and ran to warn the next wagon, while Mr. Cate hurried over to Shelly's chuck wagon to ring the triangle. Several cowboys from the dude ranch hurried to put their boots on as well.

The girls ran to the corral, where the dude ranch ponies were mixed in with the wagon train horses. "Shall we just grab anybody?" asked Lisa as the girls threaded their way through the nervous herd.

"Get a cow pony," said Carole. "They'll be easier to mount and they'll know what to do with the cattle."

The girls found three of the ponies in one corner of the corral, their noses pointed toward the cows, as if they sensed what was going on. They calmly allowed Stevie, Carole, and Lisa to hop on their backs, and they did not seem confused by the lack of a saddle and bridle.

"Okay," said Carole. "I'll let you two out of the corral, then we'll ride to the cattle together."

Carole unlatched the makeshift gate and soon all three girls were headed for the runaway herd.

"Hey, wait up!" someone called.

They looked back at the corral. Gabriel was waving at them. He'd hopped on a larger horse, but no one was there to open the gate for him. He looked around once, then dug his heels into the horse's side. The big bay bounded into a gallop and leaped over the corral fence.

"Wow," said Stevie in spite of herself as he galloped up.

"About six ranch hands are right behind me," he

called breathlessly. "They said to ride down to the top of the herd and try to head the cattle off from this direction."

"Okay," said Carole. "Let's go!"

Clutching their horses' manes, all four riders galloped into the night. They held on tightly with their legs as the wind whipped their faces. A quarter of a mile away, they could see huge numbers of cattle thundering toward them.

"Rascal Robbie said to fan out and make a lot of noise," Gabriel yelled. "That should confuse them and make them stop."

"Okay," yelled Carole back. She pointed to the left. "You and Stevie go that way. Lisa and I will go over here."

"What sort of noise are we supposed to make?" called Lisa.

"Cowboy noises, I guess." For once Gabriel seemed at a loss. "Something like this." He guided his horse to the left, threw back his head, and shrieked a loud *"Yeeeee-hiiiiiii!"* that echoed against the distant hills.

"Let's go, then!" said Carole.

Stevie veered off and rode along beside Gabriel, screaming like a banshee. Carole and Lisa galloped to the right, doing their own versions of cowboy yells. They rode straight at the oncoming herd. At first the herd kept thundering along, but then the cattle slowed

113

as they became aware of the four screaming riders rushing toward them.

"They're slowing down a little!" called Stevie, yelling over all the hoofbeats. "But they're sure not stopping!"

"Ride closer to me," answered Gabriel. "Maybe we can divide them up and push some of them in another direction."

Stevie moved closer to Gabriel, and together they rode at the left third of the herd. Carole looked over, realized what their strategy was, and did the same thing with Lisa. The two pairs of riders would split the herd into three parts, leaving the middle part for the cowboys to take care of. They all realized it was a long shot, but it was the best chance they had.

"Yeee-hiiiii!" shouted Gabriel again, urging his horse to go faster. Stevie did the same thing. So did Lisa and Carole. For a moment the herd kept roaring at them as one huge mass; then a few lead steer on Stevie and Gabriel's side began to turn off. As they turned, all the cattle behind them followed. The herd was dividing!

"Oh, wow!" Stevie yelled, watching as the cattle turned and galloped away from the camp. "It actually worked!"

"Yeah, it did!" whooped Gabriel.

They looked over at Carole and Lisa. The strategy had worked for them, too. The right-hand part of the herd had also turned and was now running east. Stevie could see Carole and Lisa waving at them in triumph. She waved back, but then looked at the smaller part of the herd that was still thundering toward the camp.

"What shall we do about them?" she asked Gabriel.

"I don't think we'll need to worry about them," he said. "Look!"

Stevie looked behind her. Bearing down on the cattle were six cowboys, waving their hats and swinging lassoes. Again the cattle slowed down and then swerved, some following Stevie's herd, others Carole's. Five of the cowboys followed them. The other rode up to Stevie and Gabriel. It was Rascal Robbie.

"I reckon my boys can take care of things now," he said. "These cattle probably won't run much farther."

Carole and Lisa rode up, out of breath. "Is everything okay?" Lisa asked.

"Everything's fine, now," said Rascal Robbie. "I was just about to say your teamwork really saved the day. Those cattle would have mashed flat everything in the camp if it hadn't been for you four. That was some fancy riding you were doing there."

Stevie reached down and gave her pony a pat.

Rascal Robbie tipped his cowboy hat. "Well, I guess I'd better run along and see what's going on. Thanks again. You're mighty brave folks." He turned his horse and rode toward the bulk of the herd. Lisa, Carole, Stevie, and Gabriel sat on their horses and watched as he faded into the night.

"Is everybody okay?" asked Carole.

"We are," said Stevie, glancing at Gabriel. "Although my throat's awfully sore from all that cowboy yelling."

"I feel like I'm covered in dust." Lisa rubbed her eyes.

"Why don't we ride over to the river?" suggested Carole. "We can give the horses a drink and go for a midnight swim."

"You guys go ahead," said Gabriel. "I'm going back to camp to report to Jeremy." He turned his horse and loped off.

"And thanks to you, too, Mr. Assistant Trail Boss," muttered Stevie.

The girls rode over to the river. The tired, sweaty ponies took long swallows of the cool water while the girls took off their jeans and waded into the river, washing away the dirt and dust from the stampeding cattle. They were floating leisurely in the deeper water when Stevie heard a strangely familiar sobbing.

"Hey!" She raised her head. "Listen! That's the same weird sound I heard just before I went to sleep!"

The girls listened. Drifting over the gurgle of the river came an ugly, gasping wail.

116

Lisa looked around nervously. "What kind of animal makes a noise like that?"

"Look!" said Carole. "Downstream on that rock! It's Eileen!"

The girls looked where Carole pointed. Huddled on a rock overhanging the river sat Eileen, yowling like a wounded cat. "Teddy!" Her heartrending sobs echoed across the water. "Oh, my poor, lost Teddy!"

"Can you believe that?" whispered Lisa. "She's probably been there all night looking for her teddy bear!"

"I can believe it," Stevie replied. "You know what else I can believe? I can believe that awful yowling is what started the stampede in the first place. That little girl and her stupid teddy bear almost got everyone killed!"

Suddenly Eileen's parents appeared. "Eileen!" her father's voice rang out sternly. "Where have you been? Everyone's been searching for you!"

"I've been down here looking for Teddy," Eileen sobbed.

"Well, you climb back up here right now! We thought you'd been killed in the stampede!"

The girls watched as Eileen climbed up the riverbank to rejoin her parents. "Thank goodness they found her," said Lisa. "Otherwise she might have stayed out here yowling and started the stampede all over again."

"Oh, I'm going to take a good swim," said Stevie, "and just wash that little creep out of my system."

With long, smooth strokes, Stevie swam upstream, then flipped over and began floating back to Carole and Lisa. She was lazily dangling her hands and arms in the water when she felt something squishy brush against her fingertips.

"Hey!" she called to her friends. "I just felt something weird. I'm going down to investigate." She dived and ran her hands along the river bottom. Tangled in some underwater branches was the distinct form of a small stuffed animal. Stevie gave the thing a yank and surfaced with it in her hand. She opened her eyes. Sure enough, it was a dripping, dirty teddy bear.

"Hey!" she cried again. "Look what I found!"

"Eileen's teddy bear!" Carole and Lisa said together.

Stevie looked at the mangy thing in disgust. "You know, it would serve her right if I just dropped this back in the river and let it float all the way to the Gulf of Mexico."

"It would," Carole agreed.

Stevie dangled the bear over the water, considering her options. She looked at it for a long moment. Then she threw it back onshore.

118

"I thought you were going to send Teddy down the river," Lisa said, surprised.

"Oh, I probably should," grumbled Stevie. "But after everything else we've done tonight, it just doesn't seem right."

They climbed out of the river and let themselves air-dry in the grass. When they were only slightly damp, they got up, took the now cool ponies back to their corral, then walked back to camp. "Let's go make our special delivery," said Stevie, turning toward Eileen's wagon. "Then let's go to bed."

The girls knocked on the back of the wagon. Eileen's father stuck his head out around the canvas flap. "Well, hello, girls," he said, sounding surprised to see them. "Can I help you?"

"Well, we were swimming in the river and found this." Stevie held up the bedraggled bear. "I think it must belong to Eileen."

"Oh, my goodness!" cried Eileen's father. "Helen! Come here! Look what these girls have found!"

Eileen's mother stuck her head out of the wagon. "Oh," she cried, tears welling up in her eyes. "Eileen's Teddy! She'll be so thrilled. Let me wake her up right now so she can thank you herself!"

"Oh, no, that's okay," Stevie said, quickly backing away from the wagon. "Eileen doesn't need to thank us.

Let her keep on sleeping. Seeing her sweet smile again tomorrow will be thanks enough!"

"Thank you so much, girls," Eileen's father said as they all backed away. "You don't know what this means to us!"

The girls turned toward their wagon. Most of the campers had gone back to bed, but a few were still up and talking about the events of the night.

"Here come the heroes!" Mr. Cate called as the girls passed by his wagon. "How does it feel to have saved the camp from certain death?"

"Actually, it feels pretty tired, Mr. Cate," Carole yawned.

Karen Nicely laughed. "Haven't you heard? We all get a holiday tomorrow! Jeremy said we can all sleep in as late as we want. And anybody who wakes you three up will have to eat dust at the end of the train for the rest of the trip!"

The girls looked at each other sleepily. "Hey," Stevie said softly, holding her hand up for a high fifteen. "All right!"

They found their camp in the same jumble they'd left it in hours before, when they'd first heard the stampede. Without bothering to straighten anything up, they collapsed into their sleeping bags and fell into a deep and dreamless sleep.

LISA WOKE UP first the next day. A scrub jay squawking in the brush near their wagon woke her, and when she opened her eyes she saw that the sun was higher in the sky than it had been any other morning they'd been on the trip. She yawned. It felt as if they'd slept forever. How nice it was of Jeremy to call a holiday after everything that had happened the night before. She wondered if Carole and Stevie had slept as soundly as she had.

"Anybody else awake?" she asked without lifting her head from her pillow.

"I am," Carole said through a deep, relaxed yawn.

"I am, too," added Stevie. "Ever since that bird

started singing." She sat up and rubbed her eyes in the morning light. "Gosh. Look how bright it is. It must be close to noon."

"Actually, it's only seven-thirty," said Carole, checking her watch. "It just feels like noon."

"Wasn't it great to sleep in?" Stevie sighed and stretched her arms.

"It was," Carole agreed. "But I think we earned it. We did an awful lot of important stuff yesterday."

"We did, didn't we?" said Lisa. "We got our wagon across the river and we saved Eileen's family's supplies and we stopped a cattle stampede."

"And I returned that dear little brat's precious teddy bear," said Stevie. "We did do a lot yesterday. No wonder I'm starving now." She unzipped her sleeping bag and stood up. "Let's go see if anything's left for breakfast."

They dressed quickly and hurried to the chuck wagon. Instead of the usual pot of steaming mush, the girls found Shelly waiting to cook them a special breakfast of flapjacks and maple syrup.

"Boss's orders." Shelly grinned as he heaped a tall stack of flapjacks on each of their plates. "Today we're celebrating a special occasion, and we're eating high on the hog, just like the pioneers would have."

"Do you know what happened to the rest of the cattle last night?" Stevie asked as Shelly ladled lots of warm maple syrup over her flapjacks.

"That cowboy Rascal Robbie came by here this morning and said they raced for another quarter mile or so, then just ran out of steam. They herded 'em back by the river and gathered up the stragglers this morning, then went on their way." Shelly chuckled. "Rascal Robbie also said to 'thank those three brave girls who helped so much last night.' "

"He thinks we're brave." Lisa looked surprised.

The girls finished their flapjacks by Shelly's campfire and hurried back to their wagon. Even though Jeremy had declared it a holiday, that didn't mean they could goof off the entire day. They still had a lot of ground to cover, and it would take most of the day to do it.

By nine o'clock everyone was ready to go. Jeremy gave a hearty "Wagons ho!" and the train began to roll west. Stevie called her customary "giddyap" to Yankee and Doodle while Lisa began to tug Veronica along behind her. Carole and Nikkia trotted easily beside them.

"You know, it feels like we've being doing this all our lives," Stevie said, watching Yankee and Doodle as they pulled smoothly against their horse collars.

"I know," said Lisa. "These clothes don't feel strange

anymore, and even Veronica seems like an old pal."
She turned and smiled at the slow-moving cow lumbering after her.

"And Nikkia's trot honestly feels smooth." Carole laughed. "I guess Starlight will feel like silk when I ride him again."

Just then Karen Nicely rode up on her buckskin mare. "How are our heroines doing today?"

"We feel great, Karen," said Carole. "How are you?"

"Actually, Shelly said I could ask a favor of you. I was wondering if you would be willing to trade a bucket of Veronica's milk for a quarter wheel of some cheddar cheese I've got."

"It's fine with me," Lisa said. She glanced back at the cow. "And I'm sure it's fine with Veronica."

"Great. I'll check back with you when we stop for lunch."

Just as Karen Nicely trotted off, Mr. Cate walked up.

"Hey, Stevie, have you heard about the new restaurant on the moon?" He grinned up at her.

"No, I haven't, Mr. Cate." Stevie raised one eyebrow.

"They say the food's great, but there's no atmosphere!" Mr. Cate threw back his head and gave a deep belly laugh.

"That's a good one, Mr. Cate," she said, chuckling.

"I knew you'd like it!" Still laughing, Mr. Cate walked over toward his wagon.

The train rolled on. The girls noticed that little Eileen was staring dejectedly out the back of her family's wagon several lengths ahead of them. "Her parents must have wised up," said Carole, "and put her in pioneer time-out."

"Good thing," Lisa replied. "Now at least they can have some fun and not worry about what kind of trouble she might be causing."

"I don't know about you guys, but I'm going to need to wash this dress pretty soon." Stevie sniffed her bodice and grimaced. "It's getting pretty ripe."

"Me too," said Lisa. "Let's wash together at the next creek we stop at. Polly Shaver brought one of those old-timey washboards with her and said we could use it anytime."

Stevie laughed. "I bet once we do our laundry with a washboard, doing it in a washing machine at home won't seem nearly so bad."

After they had traveled a few hours, Carole spotted a huge rock that jutted up from the prairie all by itself.

"Look!" She pointed to the single tall crag that broke the flat line of the horizon.

"I bet that's Miller's Rock!" cried Stevie. "I bet that's where we're going to stop for lunch today."

Just as she spoke, Jeremy took off his hat and waved

it at the rock. Slowly the wagons turned and began to roll toward it. They made good time on the dry ground, and by midday they were pulling to a halt just underneath the great boulder.

"Lunch in half an hour," Shelly called as the trekkers parked their wagons.

"Let's go," said Stevie, leaping to the ground. She and Lisa grabbed two buckets and got fresh water, while Carole brought hay for Vernonica and the horses. After Stevie had used one bucket to water the livestock, Lisa used the other to cool Yankee and Doodle down in the hot sun. As they worked, other members of the wagon train tended to their own livestock and helped each other make sure their wagons were ready for the rest of the trip. Just as the girls finished their chores, Shelly rang the triangle for lunch.

"Look at where we're eating today!" Lisa said as they followed everyone to the chuck wagon.

The girls peered over at Miller's Rock Memorial Park, where several pioneers already sat eating their lunch. A hot dog stand and souvenir shop stood at one end of a busy parking lot, surrounded by crowds of tourists. One frantic mother was trying to calm her two crying children, while another man had his entire family posing in front of the Miller's Rock historic marker as he tried to focus his camera.

126

"Gosh," said Carole as she waited in the chow line for baked beans and corn bread. "Looks like we're back in the middle of the twentieth century."

"It looks so strange, and we've only been gone for four days," said Lisa.

The girls walked to the picnic area and found an empty table next to a family of five who all wore bright orange "Cummings Exterminating—We Won't Bug You" T-shirts. The family stared at the girls as they sat down in their pioneer costumes to eat their simple meal of corn bread and beans.

"Who are they?" they heard one little girl ask her father.

"Oh, I think they're Pennsylvania Dutch," the father whispered.

The Saddle Club looked at each other and giggled.

"We could explain," Lisa suggested.

Stevie glanced over her shoulder at the man, who was splashing ketchup all over a giant order of french fries. "Forget it," she said, shaking her head. "He'd never understand."

They were just beginning to eat when a shadow fell across their table. They looked up. Gabriel stood there, his plate of lunch in his hand.

"Hi," he said, giving one of his lopsided smiles. "Could I sit with you guys?"

127

"Oh, are you sure the assistant trail boss ought to be seen eating with a bunch of womenfolk?" Stevie cracked.

"Sure, Gabriel, sit down," Carole said, nudging Stevie in the ribs. She knew as well as Stevie that Gabriel was an obnoxious jerk, but he was part of their wagon train family, so that made him *their* obnoxious jerk. And after all, they had been through a lot together.

"Have you girls had a good morning?" he asked politely, taking off his cowboy hat.

"Yes," replied Lisa. "It actually feels like we've done this all our lives."

"Well, I just wanted to make kind of an apology." He brushed his dark hair back. "I think I might have judged you guys too quickly. All three of you really did a terrific job at the stampede last night." He looked at Carole with his fierce blue eyes. "If you hadn't waked everybody up, there might have been a real disaster."

He smiled at Lisa. "And you did more than your share of turning the herd away." He swallowed. "You guys are all darn good horsewomen."

"Thanks," Stevie said loudly, enjoying the blush that suddenly turned his cheeks red.

"Yeah," Carole and Lisa said together. "Thanks."

Gabriel smiled and ate a piece of corn bread. "You know, you're such good riders, it's too bad you won't be

128

able to compete in any of the open events at the rodeo we're going to tomorrow night." He looked at Stevie and grinned. "I'm going to be in the pole racing and the calf roping. But that stuff is really guy stuff. They'll probably have a cow chip tossing contest for girls."

"A cow chip tossing contest?" Stevie felt her face flush with anger.

"Yeah," Gabriel laughed. "You know, where you take a little cow chip and see how far you can toss it. You'd be great at that, Stevie. I bet you've got quite an arm."

Stevie was speechless. Gabriel ate his last bite of lunch and stood up. "Well, I enjoyed eating with you ladies." He tipped his hat. "See you around."

They watched as he strode back to the wagons. Stevie was the first one to break the silence.

"Do you believe him?" she sputtered.

Carole giggled. "I bet he stays up nights studying his be-the-biggest-jerk-you-can-be manual."

"I don't think he studies it," fumed Stevie. "I think he wrote it!"

Suddenly Lisa stood up. "Come on, girls. Let's go back to the wagon train. It looks like Jeremy is making some kind of announcement."

They left the picnic area and hurried over to the chuck wagon, where Jeremy was talking to a group of pioneers.

"We're going to take a little break today, since we've

129

made it to Miller's Rock. Our next campsite isn't far away, so we'll be staying here until midafternoon. You can spend the next couple of hours resting or relaxing, or you can climb Miller's Rock if you want. It's a moderate to strenuous climb that takes about two hours, round trip. Just make sure you're back here by three, ready to roll."

The girls looked at the rock. They could already hear Gabriel's voice behind them, advising Karen Nicely on the best way to climb in pioneer clothes.

"What do you think?" Stevie asked, squinting at the tall, craggy rock glowing red in the sun.

"We could try it," said Carole. "It would be neat to be able to say we'd done it."

"We could also relax." Lisa frowned at the sharp granite face of the rock. "I mean, we kind of killed ourselves yesterday and last night."

"You're right," said Stevie. "I vote we take our chances on the ground. I mean, something even more exciting could happen down here."

"That's fine with me," said Carole. "For once, why don't we just sit under a shady tree and wait for the next exciting thing to come along?"

13

THE GIRLS FOUND a shady tree close to their wagon with a good view of Miller's Rock. While they sprawled on the ground watching several pioneers attempting the climb, their animals rested nearby. Veronica dozed in the bright sunshine, and the horses browsed in the thick prairie grass. From a distance, Mr. Cate's version of "The Tennessee Waltz" floated on the air, and a group of pioneer children ran past them in a fast game of capture the flag. Little Eileen was nowhere to be seen.

"You know, this is really nice." Stevie sighed and relaxed against the tree. "Even though I didn't know any of these people four days ago, I feel completely at home."

"I do, too," said Carole, plucking a blade of grass. "I feel that together we could handle most anything."

"It's Miller's Rock." Lisa smiled mysteriously.

"Huh?" Stevie and Carole said together.

"It's Miller's Rock. Remember what Jeremy said? He guaranteed that by the time we reached Miller's Rock we'd be totally different people. Well, here we are. Totally changed at Miller's Rock. And it only took four days."

"Plus a tipped-over wagon and a stampede and a know-it-all assistant trail boss and a little brat who couldn't get over her missing teddy bear," Stevie reminded them.

"And also the departure of Deborah," said Carole.

"That's true. But you know, I think everybody else has changed, too," said Lisa. "I mean, everybody seems more helpful and more interested in seeing that other people are okay."

"You're right," Carole agreed. "I don't even think Gabriel is as bad as he was. He can be nice when he wants to be."

Lisa smiled. "He wasn't nearly as obnoxious at lunch today. And he *does* have gorgeous eyes!"

"Oh, don't be too sure," said Stevie. "Aren't you forgetting the fact that he was taunting us about the rodeo?" She imitated his words. " 'I'm riding in the races. You girls will have to do the cow chip toss.' "

132

She snorted. "If that's not obnoxious, I don't know what is."

Carole frowned. "Stevie, give him credit. Did you see the jump he took last night? Over the corral fence with no saddle or bridle? He rides awfully well."

"Oh, he just got lucky," Stevie muttered. For some reason the idea of Gabriel's being a good rider made her mad all over again. She couldn't believe that Lisa and Carole didn't think he was obnoxious anymore. If Gabriel wasn't obnoxious, that would mean that Phil's new girlfriend wasn't obnoxious, either. And if she wasn't obnoxious, what was she? Did she even exist? Stevie scratched her head in dismay. There was so much about Phil's trip she didn't know, and she didn't like the idea of not knowing.

"I've got an idea," said Lisa. "Since we've made it to Miller's Rock and become true pioneers, let's drink a toast." She uncapped her leather canteen. "To The Saddle Club. We can accomplish anything when we work together!"

"To The Saddle Club," Stevie added, "which still has more to accomplish. We have to beat the assistant trail boss at his own game. We'll show him a thing or two at the rodeo!"

Carole laughed. "Stevie! You're on the wrong vacation. You should be reenacting the gold rush to California."

"Yeah, Stevie," giggled Lisa. "Or maybe the Pony Express. You could have been the first one there with the most mail."

Stevie grinned. "Well, maybe I am slightly competitive. But isn't winning something you want to win what teamwork is all about?"

"I suppose," laughed Lisa. She held her canteen in the air and repeated, "To The Saddle Club!"

Stevie and Carole clunked their leather canteens against Lisa's. "To tomorrow," added Stevie. "When The Saddle Club will teach the assistant trail boss a thing or two!"

The girls took a sip from their canteens. Just then Shelly's triangle broke the still air. Their minivacation had ended.

"The trail leads westward again," said Carole.

"Right," Stevie said with a grin. "Westward to the sunset, westward to the rodeo, and westward to all points beyond!"

THE BET'S ON!

"You know, I've been thinking about this bet we've got going," said Gabriel.

"Oh?" Stevie's heart began to beat faster. Maybe Gabriel was about to chicken out!

"Yeah. In fact, I've been thinking about it all day."

Stevie smiled to herself. He was trying to find a way to weasel out of it! Maybe there was a chance they could forget this whole thing. "And?" she asked hopefully.

"And I've just decided what I'm going to make you do when I win!" he announced gleefully.

"When you *win?*" she repeated as she felt her face heat up with both anger and disappointment.

"Yeah. When I win. It's really going to be great!"

"Well, before you start enjoying your little dare too much, you'd better start worrying about what I'm going to make you do when *I* win," retorted Stevie quickly. "It'll go down in the annals of rodeo history!"

the
Saddle Club

Wagon Trail +
Quarter Horse

Bonnie Bryant

RANDOM HOUSE AUSTRALIA

*I would like to express my special thanks
to Sallie Bissell for her help
in the writing of this book.*

"JUST A FEW MORE minutes and I'll be there!" Stevie whispered happily as she guided her horse through a shallow creek of gurgling blue water. It had been a perfect day—the weather had been warm, the sunlight had sparkled, and a gentle breeze had carried the smell of blooming wildflowers. Now, as the sun was beginning to set, the whole western half of the sky glowed with a rosy light.

"It's going to be so romantic," Stevie anticipated out loud. "He'll be waiting for me at Pioneer Rock. Then we'll walk our horses along the mesa trail; then, just as the sun disappears below the horizon, he'll take me in his arms and . . ." She closed her eyes with a shiver of delight, then sat forward in the saddle and urged Belle faster. "Come on, Belle, let's hurry! We don't want to be late!"

1

Stevie looked down at Belle. It seemed funny. She couldn't remember bringing her own horse on this trip, but it was Belle she was riding. Her mount had the same thick, dark mane, the same easy canter, and the same familiar whinny Stevie had come to love. She was definitely on board Belle, and Belle was taking her to meet Phil.

Wait. Stevie frowned as Belle cantered faster. Wasn't Phil out rafting on a river with his family? Hadn't he invited Stevie to go along? That she remembered clearly. Now, if Phil was out on some river, then who was Belle taking her to meet?

Suddenly Belle began to slow down. They were nearing Pioneer Rock, but oddly, someone had constructed an ice cream shop there. A familiar red-and-white awning shaded the tables and chairs in the front window. Stevie blinked in amazement. It was TD's, their hangout in Virginia! A tall figure was waiting for her by the front door. *There's Phil*, she thought, smiling as Belle carried her closer. *I can tell by the way he stands with his hands in his pockets.*

Stevie looked more closely at the figure by the door. *Wait. Phil's not that tall, and his hair's not that dark, and he never wears a cowboy hat.* Suddenly she pulled hard on Belle's right rein. Phil wasn't standing there waiting for her! Gabriel was!

"No!" Stevie cried, sitting up straight, her heart pounding. Droplets of cold sweat ran down her neck, and for a

2

moment she couldn't catch her breath. Where was she? Where was Phil? And where was Belle?

She looked around and forced herself to take several deep, slow breaths. Carole and Lisa lay on either side of her, their sleeping bags pulled up to their chins. Ten covered wagons made a large circle around them, and in the middle of that circle, Stevie could see the orange glow of a banked campfire.

"Now I remember," she whispered. "We're here, out West, reenacting part of the pioneers' journey on the Oregon Trail." A week before, Deborah Hale, Max Regnery's wife, had asked The Saddle Club to join her on this trip and help her do field research for an article she was supposed to write. Deborah had had to return unexpectedly to Virginia, but Jeremy Barksdale, the wagon master, had offered to take The Saddle Club girls under his wing so that they could complete the trip. Now here they were, wearing genuine pioneer clothes, eating genuine pioneer food, driving one covered wagon, three horses, and a cow along part of the Oregon Trail.

"Whew!" Stevie wiped the sweat from the back of her neck as she remembered with a shudder how it felt to have Belle carrying her toward obnoxious Gabriel. "Thank goodness that was only a dream." She plumped up her pillow. "Or I should say nightmare."

Stevie and the other girls had met Gabriel their first day out West. Though he was just another participant in the wagon train reenactment, Jeremy had made him assistant trail boss because he knew so much history about the Oregon Trail. Gabriel was tall and handsome and rode like a dream, but Stevie thought he was the biggest jerk on the planet. Throughout the trip his know-it-all attitude had been almost unbearable. Once he'd given her a long lecture when he'd mistakenly thought she was trying to race her team of horses; then he'd tried to outdo her in ghost-story telling; then he'd informed her that the only rodeo event she was fit to enter was the cow chip tossing contest!

"Jerk," Stevie muttered as she settled back down in her sleeping bag. "Now he's even intruding in my dreams. If this keeps up, I'll be afraid to go to sleep!" She rolled over and closed her eyes. She needed to get some rest. On the wagon train their days started at five-thirty and did not end until sunset.

She took a few more deep breaths and tried to concentrate on something pleasant—like Phil. *He's so cute*, Stevie thought with a smile. *He's got such pretty green eyes and such a nice smile*. Suddenly Gabriel's face appeared before her—his deep blue eyes sparkling as he smiled, and—Stevie shook her head, evaporated Gabriel, and again pictured Phil. *He's got such a nice laugh*, she thought. *And he looks so good on his horse, Teddy*. Again Gabriel materialized. He, too, had a nice laugh, when he was laughing *with* her instead of *at* her, and he sat his quarter horse as if he'd been born on it. Stevie sighed and tried to force her thoughts back to all the wonderful times she'd had with Phil when suddenly the cute little dimple in Gabriel's cheek flashed through her head.

"This just isn't working!" she said, more awake than ever. She turned over and plunged her fist into her pillow. "I'm going to try counting sheep." She closed her eyes and pictured sheep leaping over the corral fence. Their white coats were fluffy and they baaed as they leaped through the air, but she found herself wondering where they would go and what they would do, and whether they would be able to find their way back to the corral. Her eyes flew open again. She sighed once more and rolled over.

"Maybe this time I'll try horses," she whispered as she punched her pillow a second time. "I'll start with the first horse I ever knew and work my way up." She pictured the first horse she had ever climbed on—a Shetland pony named Brownie. She had been three years old, and her mother had snapped a picture of her. *Wonder what ever happened to Brownie*, Stevie thought, her mind veering off in another direction. *I wonder if he's still giving little kids rides at that carnival . . . I wonder if he still has those shaggy blond bangs*. She'd just begun to worry if they were giving an old pony like Brownie the right kind of feed when she opened her eyes and sat up in her sleeping bag once again.

"This is terrible," she whispered, looking over at Carole and Lisa as they slept peacefully under the starry sky. "If I try to think of Phil, I think of Gabriel. If I try to count

5

sheep, I start wondering where they go when they leave the corral. And when I think of all the horses I've known, I worry about what's become of them." She looked at the ghostly shapes of the covered-wagon tops. *I wonder what the pioneers counted when they had insomnia. Probably all the aches and pains they got from riding in their wagons*, she decided, wiggling around to make her sore rear end more comfortable.

Suddenly she grinned. "I've got it," she whispered. "The perfect solution. It's endless and boring enough to put me right to sleep." She fluffed her pillow for the final time and rolled over on her side. Smiling, she closed her eyes and began counting softly to herself.

"The first annoying thing Gabriel did was stand up and brag about how only brave *men* opened up the West. . . . The second annoying thing Gabriel did was to insinuate that I didn't know how to hitch up a team of horses to a wagon. . . . The third annoying thing Gabriel did was to tell me that in the old days menfolk never relied on womenfolk. . . . The fourth annoying thing . . ." Stevie was just about to recount what the fourth annoying thing was when her eyelids fluttered once and she finally fell into a deep and dreamless sleep.

"STEVIE!" THE NEXT THING Stevie heard was a voice, calling from somewhere above her head.

"Hmmmpf," she replied, snuggling back down in her

sleeping bag and trying to reenter the dream she was having about Phil.

"Stevie, wake up! We're going to delay the whole wagon train if we don't get going!"

Stevie opened one eye. Lisa stood above her, already wearing the pioneer dress she'd worn throughout the trip. Her hair was combed back behind her ears, and her blue eyes looked rested from a good night's sleep.

"What time is it?" Stevie croaked.

"It's almost six. Everyone's already eating breakfast."

Stevie rubbed her eyes. Carole and Lisa, dressed in their pioneer clothes, were looking down at her. "You guys go on. I'll catch up to you in a few minutes."

"You won't go back to sleep, will you?" Carole asked dubiously.

"No." Stevie shook her head. "I'm awake. I'll be there as soon as I get dressed."

Stevie crawled out of her sleeping bag while Carole and Lisa walked over to the chuck wagon. On the far side of the circle she could see Shelly Bean, the camp cook, dishing out the hot cornmeal mush that everyone ate for breakfast. Quickly she rolled up her sleeping bag and climbed into the wagon. After she stashed her pillow and blankets, she pulled on her own scratchy dress and brushed her teeth in the bucket of water that Lisa had hung behind the driver's seat. Stevie gave her hair a quick brushing, then jumped out of the wagon. As she walked over to join her friends for breakfast, she noticed that an air of excitement hung over the wagon train. Today was their last full day on the trail. That afternoon they would roll into Clinchport and start preparing for the local rodeo.

"Morning, Stevie," Polly Shaver called from the back of her wagon. Polly was a dance instructor from Cleveland and one of the new friends the girls had made on their trip. She pointed her camera at Stevie, then lowered it again. "I was going to take your picture, but you look a little tired."

"I didn't sleep too well," Stevie replied with a yawn.

"You must have been dreaming about the rodeo," Polly teased.

"I wish." Stevie shook her head as she walked over to Lisa and Carole. *More like I was having nightmares about the dumb old assistant trail boss*, she thought glumly.

"Hi, Stevie. Glad you made it." Carole stepped forward as Stevie slipped into line behind her. Carole wore her long dark hair in a single braid so that her cowboy hat would fit easily on her head. "Did you have trouble sleeping last night? I vaguely remember you sitting up and mumbling something about counting sheep."

"I had a terrible night last night," grumbled Stevie as she grabbed a tin cup and plate. "Sheep were only a few of the things I tried to count."

The breakfast line inched forward. "Why, here come

8

my three favorite girls from Virginia." Shelly grinned through his curly gray beard as the girls neared his steaming pot of mush. "Step right up here and let me give you a good, hot breakfast. You'll need lots of energy if we're gonna roll into Clinchport today."

Shelly loaded their plates. Then they dipped out some milk from the bucket on the chuck wagon and sat down close to the fire. Though the sun was up, last night's chill had not left the air. The girls ate quickly and hurried back to their wagon to get ready to go. Lisa packed up their gear while Stevie and Carole went to the corral to get Yankee, Doodle, and Nikkia, their horses. The girls had just started to lead them back to the wagon when they saw Gabriel walking toward them.

"Oh, brother," Stevie sighed as she pulled Yankee and Doodle along behind her. "Here comes Mr. Know-It-All."

"Maybe he won't be such a jerk today," Carole whispered, holding Nikkia's halter as Gabriel sauntered up to them wearing his usual smug smile.

"Hi, ladies," he said, tipping his cowboy hat. "I noticed you were late for breakfast. Is your wagon going to be ready for the final push to Clinchport?"

"It is," snapped Stevie.

"Well, you'll be driving behind Mr. Cate's wagon today," he said. "It's your turn to ride drag."

"No kidding," Stevie muttered.

9

Gabriel smirked. "And you might want to consider wearing a bonnet and a bandanna over your nose. I'd hate for all that nasty dust to mess up your hair."

"Thanks for thinking of us, Mr. Assistant Trail Boss," Stevie said. "I don't know what we womenfolk would do without you."

"My pleasure," he said, striding off to help Karen Nicely with her horse's bridle.

"Ugh." Stevie clenched her fists. "Sometimes he makes me so mad I don't know what to do."

"Just take it easy, Stevie," said Carole. "We've only got one more day to put up with him as assistant trail boss."

"You're right," Stevie said as she led the two big quarter horses to the wagon traces. "How bad can it be?"

A few minutes later, The Saddle Club was ready to roll. Stevie took her usual place driving the wagon, and Carole rode Nikkia alongside. Lisa was in charge of Veronica, the milk cow, who more or less ambled along behind her. In the past five days the girls had grown accustomed to their pioneer jobs and now did them easily and well. Stevie watched for Jeremy's signal to roll forward as she gathered the reins in her hand.

"Oooh, do you have to ride in the back today?" a small voice called. Stevie peered down in front of the horses. There stood Eileen, the eight-year-old brat whose wailing over a lost teddy bear had caused a cattle stampede two nights before. It was only through Carole's quick thinking and The Saddle Club's great teamwork with Gabriel that

10

an entire herd of rampaging longhorns had been diverted away from the wagon train encampment.

"Yes, we are," said Stevie. "And I thought you were supposed to be riding in the back of your parents' wagon."

"I was," replied Eileen. "But I apologized so hard for everything I'd done and I cried so many tears over it that they let me out." She gave Stevie a sly grin. "They said now I can go anywhere I want."

"Oh?" Stevie raised one eyebrow.

"Yes. I could even stand here in front of your wagon all day if I wanted to."

"You might get run over," Stevie pointed out.

"I would not! You wouldn't dare run over me!"

"Oh, brother," Stevie said to herself. She was just about to reply when Eileen's mother called to her daughter in an irritated voice. In a flash, the little girl had turned and was running toward her own wagon. "Saved by the bell," Stevie muttered.

Slowly the wagons began to move forward. Stevie popped Yankee and Doodle's reins and took her place at the end of the line. Farther ahead, Lisa and Veronica were posing for Polly's camera, and Carole had ridden Nikkia forward to help someone sort out a nervous horse. At the head of the wagon train, Stevie could see Gabriel, leading the way.

"Why am I dreaming about him, of all people?" she began to wonder out loud. She frowned. "I don't even like him. And if I'm dreaming about somebody I don't even like, then who in the world is Phil dreaming about?" Ever since the trip had begun, Stevie had fought a niggling worry that Phil might have met a new girl on his rafting trip—a cuter, smarter, more fun girl than she was. Even though Carole and Lisa had told her that she was being silly and that it was just not possible, she hadn't been able to shake the uneasy feeling from her mind.

She yawned, then clucked to Yankee and Doodle. "If I'm dreaming about somebody I can't stand, then Phil must be having cyberoptic, digitized visions of his dream girl," Stevie said grumpily. "He's probably so sleepy every morning, he can barely stay on his raft!"

THE WAGON TRAIN rolled into Clinchport late that afternoon, making its usual wide circle on a grassy plateau that overlooked the rodeo grounds. Stevie drove Yankee and Doodle up just behind Mr. Cate's wagon and pulled on the parking brake.

"I guess that's where the action's going to be." Mr. Cate hopped off his wagon and shielded his eyes as he gazed down at the flat plain where a wide horse-racing track adjoined a large arena. Red, white, and blue bunting hung from the grandstand and American flags fluttered festively from every available pole. He grinned over at Stevie. "Are you excited about the rodeo?"

"I sure am," Stevie replied as she began to unhitch Yankee and Doodle. "But right now I'm more excited about not having to drive that bumpy wagon anymore."

"They could use some shock absorbers, couldn't they?" Mr. Cate drawled in his soft Alabama accent. He rubbed his back. "Maybe the pioneers were just better padded than we are."

The wagon train made camp. Working smoothly as a team, The Saddle Club soon had their horses unhitched and their campsite ready for the night. Carole unsaddled Nikkia and helped Stevie take Yankee and Doodle to the makeshift corral, while Lisa gave Veronica some hay and brought a fresh bucket of water from the creek. They had just finished their chores when Jeremy's voice rang out from the center of the encampment.

"Congratulations, all you pioneers!" he said as everyone gathered around him. "We've made it to the end of the trail, and our worst catastrophe was the dousing of one teddy bear!" Everyone laughed except Eileen, who crossed her arms and pouted.

Jeremy continued, "We can relax and enjoy ourselves now, but I wanted to remind you that the day after tomorrow the town of Clinchport is hosting a rodeo. If some of you now expert horsemen want to try your luck at calf roping or steer wrestling—well, as part of your Wagons West experience, a local stable will provide horses to anyone who wants to give it a try." He grinned. "I would suggest first, though, that you check out what events they're having. If you still want to participate, the Rocking S stable is directly behind the west grandstand. Just

14

tell the head wrangler you're with Wagons West, and he'll help you choose a horse. Any questions?"

Karen Nicely held up her hand. "What if we don't want to ride in the rodeo? I'm still sore from riding all day on the trail."

Jeremy chuckled. "Then you can join me in the grandstand and watch while your fellow pioneers bust some broncos."

"Or some other parts of their own anatomies," Mr. Cate added with a smile.

Everyone laughed again, and then the crowd broke up. Though there would be several more hours of daylight, most people returned to their wagons. The Saddle Club, however, headed straight for the rodeo grounds.

"Let's go choose our horses first," said Stevie, pulling up the hem of her long brown pioneer dress and hurrying down the grassy slope.

"Why?" asked Lisa as she jogged along behind. "We don't even know what events they're having."

"Because if we get good horses first, we can win anything. If we sign up for the events first and wind up with plugs, then we're doomed before we've even started."

"Oh, Stevie," Carole laughed. "Only you would come up with a strategy like that."

They hurried across the large arena, which had been covered with loose, fine dirt. Though it was dusty to walk

15

on, the dirt would cushion the falls the rodeo riders took from the bucking broncos and gyrating bulls. The girls threaded their way through the west grandstand, then crossed the racetrack over to the Rocking S ranch, a long log building that had several horses tied in front.

"Howdy." A tall cowboy wearing short-fringed chaps greeted them as they entered the piney-smelling stable. "I'm Pete Parsons," he said, his thick black mustache drooping over his mouth as he talked. "Can I help you?"

"We're with Wagons West," explained Stevie, "and we'd like horses for the rodeo."

"You would, eh?" The cowboy smiled. "You ever ridden horses before?"

"Yes," replied Carole. "Back in Virginia we ride practically every day."

"And we've all ridden Western before, too," Lisa added.

"Well, then I guess you know what you're doing. Come on back here with me and I'll show you what we've got. We raise mostly quarter horses at this barn."

The girls followed Pete to a small corral behind the stable. Half a dozen muscular quarter horses grazed contentedly in the long green grass, their tails lazily swishing at the few flies that buzzed around them. About twenty feet away two other cowboys leaned against the fence, looking over the same horses. Stevie made a choking noise. One of the cowboys was Gabriel!

16

"I don't believe it," she muttered in frustration. "It's like wherever we go, he's there first!"

Gabriel glanced over and saw the girls. "Hi, ladies." He smiled and tipped his hat again. "Are you here to choose horses for the rodeo?"

"We are," said Stevie. "How about you?"

He nodded. "I can't decide between that sorrel with the blaze and the palomino."

"Unless you're a mighty good rider, I wouldn't choose the sorrel," the other cowboy advised. "Tumbleweed's a handful."

"Then I'll take Tumbleweed," cried Stevie, flashing a triumphant grin at Gabriel.

"Are you sure you're that good a rider, miss?" Pete Parsons frowned with concern.

"I'm sure I'm just as good as he is," Stevie replied, nodding at Gabriel.

"Hey, whatever." Gabriel shrugged. "I was going to choose the palomino, anyway. In a rodeo you need a horse you can depend on, not one that might go loco on you."

"Oh, I don't think Tumbleweed will go loco on me," Stevie assured him as she eyed the horse's powerfully built hindquarters. Tumbleweed looked at her and tossed his head as if he knew she was talking about him. "Maybe he would with someone less experienced, but I think I can handle him."

17

Pete and the other cowboy shook their heads while Lisa and Carole just rolled their eyes. A few minutes later, they decided on horses of their own—Lisa chose a tall gray horse named Ghost, and Carole decided on Pogo, a husky black-and-white pinto mare. After that the girls hurried to the arena to sign up for the events they would ride in.

"I hope they have barrel racing," said Lisa.

"Me too," Carole replied. "That's the one rodeo event we've done before."

"And we know how good we are at it," laughed Stevie.

The sign-up area was in the office under the grandstand. Various sheets of rodeo information lay on a long table. The girls studied the lists of events carefully. Everything was divided by age, and anyone between twelve and eighteen could ride in the five junior events.

"Let's see." Carole peered at the lists. "We've got barrel racing, calf roping, pole bending, goat wrestling, and a quarter-mile race."

"And a barbecue dinner with awards for the top riders afterward," Lisa read over her shoulder.

"And no all-girl cow chip tossing!" crowed Stevie. "Great!"

"What shall we sign up for?" Carole grabbed the pencil that was tied to the table and looked at her friends.

"Let's sign up for everything," suggested Stevie. "I can see the headlines now: 'Pine Hollow Riders Sweep Clinchport Rodeo!' "

Carole laughed. "Come on, Stevie, that's impossible. We can't do all five events. In the first place, we'd spend the whole day just running around the grounds, and in the second place, no single horse could do all those events. Most cowboys ride several horses in a rodeo."

"I guess you're right," Stevie agreed reluctantly.

"Let's all do barrel racing, since we're good at it, and then let's each sign up for one other event, just for fun," said Lisa. "That way we can still hang out with the pioneers some and watch the adult events."

Stevie shrugged. "Sounds good to me." She looked at the sign-up sheets. "I think I'll do barrel racing and the quarter-mile race. After all, we're riding quarter horses. That's what they were bred to do."

"Then I'll take barrel racing and pole bending." Carole laughed. "I've never bent a pole before. It should be fun."

Lisa frowned. "I guess I'll take barrel racing and goat wrestling. After wrestling with Veronica for the past week, I should be able to take care of one measly little goat."

"Well, let me tell you that goat wrestling is a little different than leading one old milk cow across the prairie," a voice said behind her. They turned to see Gabriel, smiling smugly, a lariat slung over his shoulder.

"What do you know about it?" Stevie said, crossing her arms. "How many goats have you wrestled?"

"Enough to know that you have to be fast and strong and not afraid to get dirty," snapped Gabriel. "It's a whole

19

lot different from old girly barrel racing. Anybody who's smart enough to hang on a horse could do that."

"And I guess you think we're just that smart?" Stevie asked.

Gabriel shrugged. "Maybe. I have my doubts about the other events, though. Girls always worry that they'll fall off and mess up their hair or tear their clothes or that they'll hurt their horses if they make them go fast." He snorted and shook his head. "Girls just aren't strong enough or fast enough to do well at rodeoing."

Stevie's eyes flashed. "You want to bet on that?" she cried.

"Sure," said Gabriel, his cheeks suddenly growing red. "I'll make a bet with you. We'll go one on one. You enter all five events on Tumbleweed and I'll enter all five events on my palomino, Napoleon. That way we'll find out who the better rider is once and for all."

"Hey, that's crazy," said Carole. "That's not fair to the horses. They'll be exhausted."

"Sure it is," replied Gabriel. "These aren't your pampered little English hunters. These are tough Western quarter horses."

"But wait, you guys," Lisa protested. "Remember we're on this trip to have fun and re-create some history, not kill each other at a rodeo."

Gabriel smiled at her. "Your buddy here is the one who wants to bet." He turned back to Stevie. "Well?" he asked again. "How about it?"

"You're on!" cried Stevie. She stuck out her hand to seal the bet. Gabriel shook it as Lisa and Carole looked on in horror.

"All five events on the same horse," Stevie repeated. "And may the best rider win."

"I CAN'T GET over how he thinks we're scared we'll mess up our hair!" Stevie fumed the next morning as she pulled on her regular blue jeans. The girls were dressing inside their wagon, and for the first time all week they were not putting on pioneer clothes but their everyday riding gear.

"Stevie, you need to calm down about this," said Carole. "You tossed and turned all night, always muttering something about Gabriel."

"I did not!" Stevie cried.

"Yes, you did, Stevie. I heard you." Lisa dipped her toothbrush in their bucket of water. "Just listen to yourself right now. We haven't even had breakfast yet and you're already grumbling about him."

"He is just such a jerk!" Stevie jammed her shirttail into her jeans.

"Yes, he is," Carole agreed. "But you can't let jerks talk you into doing things that are crazy and maybe dangerous. You've only been in one rodeo event in your entire life, and now you're betting that tomorrow you'll win everything from pole bending to goat wrestling. I wish you would just calm down and think about it a minute. You could get hurt doing all those things."

"I know, I know," said Stevie, raking a comb through her tousled hair. "It is crazy, but I just can't stand the idea of that nitwit guy thinking he's a better rider than me."

"Stevie, he may not be better than you, but admit it— he is an awfully good rider," Lisa said. "Remember how he jumped that horse bareback, *and* in the dark, the night of the stampede? Why don't you go find him this morning and just tell him you've changed your mind?"

"I could never do that!" Stevie said. "Anyway, he just got lucky over that fence. It wasn't all that high."

"Okay, okay." Lisa returned her toothbrush to her backpack. "I give up. Let's go eat breakfast now. We can discuss what a lucky rider Gabriel is over a nice bowl of hot mush."

A few minutes later the girls were sitting by the campfire, eating their mush. Shelly Bean had greeted them warmly as they came through the chow line, and for once Gabriel was not in sight.

"Why don't we go for a ride after breakfast?" suggested Lisa. "We need to get to know our horses before the rodeo tomorrow."

23

"Good idea," Carole said. "It'll be great to do some fun riding again. Nikkia's a good horse, but he and I mostly just plugged along with the wagon train."

Suddenly little Eileen appeared, still dressed in her pioneer outfit. "How come you're not wearing your pioneer clothes?" she demanded, her hands on her hips. "That's against the rules."

"Because we're going to be in the rodeo," explained Stevie. "You can't ride in a barrel race wearing a pioneer dress."

"I'm going to tell Jeremy!" Eileen wagged her finger at them. "It's against the rules for you not to wear pioneer clothes at all times, and it's not fair to everybody else!" With that she turned and ran toward her own wagon, shrieking for Jeremy at the top of her lungs.

Carole shook her head as she watched Eileen run away. "That kid is unbelievable."

"I feel kind of sorry for her," said Lisa. "I mean, if she's this obnoxious now, just think what she'll be like when she grows up."

"Ugh." Stevie shuddered. "I don't *even* want to think about it. Let's go ride."

They washed their breakfast dishes and headed toward the stable. They were just strolling down to the rodeo grounds when Stevie suddenly stopped. "Look!" She pointed to someone bent low over a horse that was thundering down one side of the track. "It's him! He's practicing already! He's racing the quarter-mile on Napoleon and it's barely sunup!"

Carole and Lisa looked where Stevie pointed. Sure enough, Napoleon was galloping around the track, his long flaxen tail flying in the wind.

"Do you believe that?" Stevie cried, running down the hill. "He must have started practicing at dawn!" She turned to Lisa and Carole. "Come on! There's not a moment to lose!"

The girls hurried down to the stable. Pete, the cowboy they'd met the day before, had put the horses they'd chosen in three separate stalls, so all the girls had to do was brush them and saddle them up.

"They're down thataway." Pete pointed to the left side of the stable. "And their gear is in the room next to the hayloft stairs. You'll see their names above their saddles."

"Thanks, Pete!" the girls called as they headed to their horses.

"You girls be careful." Pete looked at Stevie and frowned. "Don't use your spurs on Tumbleweed unless you want him to take off like a rocket."

"I'm going to need a rocket for that quarter-mile race," said Stevie.

Pete chuckled. "Then I think you may have gotten just what you need."

When they reached their horses, Ghost and Pogo were

busily munching hay, and Tumbleweed had stuck his head over the stall door.

"Do you think Tumbleweed might bite or kick you, Stevie?" Lisa asked.

"I don't care what he does to me," Stevie said, "as long as he wins those events."

Lisa and Carole exchanged worried frowns. Then each girl entered her horse's stall and began to get acquainted.

Stevie opened Tumbleweed's door quietly, looking down at the stable floor and speaking to him in a soft voice. She rubbed his nose only after she'd heard him give an inviting whinny, and then she looked up and smiled at him. His brown eyes seemed to twinkle back at her, and soon she was rubbing his back and legs, getting him accustomed to her touch.

"How are you doing, Stevie?" Carole called as she gave Pogo a good scratch behind the ears.

"I'm doing fine," Stevie said, gingerly lifting Tumbleweed's front hoof. "Tumbleweed seems like a real sweetheart."

"No kicking? No biting? No foaming at the mouth?" Lisa asked as she began to comb Ghost's silky gray mane.

"Not so far," Stevie replied. "Like Pete said, I guess it must be a spur thing."

"Ha, ha, ha," someone laughed outside the stalls. "Maybe it's a spur-of-the-moment thing!"

The girls looked out to see who was talking to them. A tall woman with bright red hair stood there. She wore tight-fitting jeans and a bright tie-dyed T-shirt with a green sequined vest that read "San Antonio Sal" across the front.

"Sorry," she said, grinning broadly. "I guess I couldn't resist a pun like that."

"It's okay," laughed Carole. "We're just used to Stevie being in charge of the pun department."

"Stevie?" The woman frowned.

"Yeah, me." Stevie smiled. "I'm Stevie Lake. These are my friends Carole Hanson and Lisa Atwood."

"Howdy," the woman replied. "I'm San Antonio Sal. Y'all must be here for the rodeo."

"We are," said Lisa. "We're with Wagons West."

"That's great," Sal said. "I'm here for the rodeo, too."

"Are you a rider?" Carole blinked at the wild colors of Sal's outfit.

"Shoot, no." Sal threw her head back and gave a deep belly laugh. "I gave up rodeoing years ago. Got too hard on my back, and also my backside. Now I'm a clown. Me and my partners, the Texarkana Twins, are supposed to work the junior events here tomorrow."

"Really?" Lisa's eyes grew wide. "Are the Texarkana Twins here, too?"

"Nope. They're driving up from Donnersville tonight. My horse Sadie and I came up here early, just to check things out." She grinned at the girls, whose horses were now saddled up and ready to go. "Are y'all going on a trail ride?"

"No," said Stevie. "We're going to the arena to practice. We've got a lot to learn and not a whole lot of time to learn it in."

"Well, don't let me keep you from your labors. Sadie and I may see you out in the ring a little later."

The girls led their horses into the arena. Gabriel was gone, so they had the place to themselves. They led each horse to the middle of the big ring and carefully mounted up. Ghost turned in a little circle when Lisa mounted, but Pogo stood quietly while Carole climbed on board. Lisa and Carole waited to see what Tumbleweed and Stevie would do.

"Here goes nothing," Stevie said, gathering her reins and planting her left foot in the stirrup.

"Good luck," Carole called.

Stevie hoisted herself up and threw her right leg over Tumbleweed. The horse stood as docilely as any of the horses did at Pine Hollow; then he arched his neck and did a little dance, as if he were eager to tackle anything Stevie might have in mind.

"I think this horse is terrific," Stevie said, giving Tumbleweed a pat on the neck. "He sure behaves for me."

"Maybe he realizes he's carrying the Amazon warrior queen of the West," Lisa said, chuckling.

"You can laugh now," said Stevie, "but you're going to love it when I beat Gabriel in all five events tomorrow!"

"Well, let's see what these guys can do," said Carole, urging Pogo into a trot.

28

They warmed up in the arena, practicing their lopes and turns and lead changes. All three of the horses had the surefootedness quarter horses are known for, and all seemed to be willing and responsive mounts.

"I think we chose pretty well." Carole pulled up in the center of the ring to give Pogo a breather.

"Me too," said Lisa. "Ghost is a super horse!"

"Hi, everybody!" a voice called from the sideline. "Y'all look pretty good out there!"

The girls turned. San Antonio Sal loped toward them, riding a beautiful leopard-spotted Appaloosa. "I believe you must have ridden once or twice before," she said, pulling up beside them.

"Well, yes, we do ride a lot." Carole smiled, pleased that Sal could see they weren't total tenderfeet.

"Practically every day," added Stevie.

Sal pushed her bright orange cowboy hat back on her head. "I can tell. All of you ride wonderfully well. What events are you doing in the rodeo?"

The girls looked at each other. "Well, Carole and I are just doing two each," Lisa said. "Stevie's going to be in all five."

"All five?" Sal's eyebrows shot up in surprise as she looked at Stevie. "Have you ever done all five of these events before?"

"No," Stevie admitted sheepishly. "But I believe you can do anything you want to if you want to bad enough."

"This boy on our wagon train, our assistant trail boss,

thinks men can do everything better than women," Carole explained. "He sort of dared Stevie to compete in all five events."

"I see," Sal said thoughtfully. She looked at Stevie, then grinned. "Well, good for you, girl. I say go get 'em! You'll just have to show that boy whose hog ate the cabbage!"

"You don't know anything about pole bending, do you?" Stevie asked.

Sal laughed. "Why, I sure do. Pole bending is just riding in and out around a string of poles stuck in the ground. Riders as good as you won't have a bit of trouble with pole bending if you remember one thing: Straighten up in the saddle a little bit as you go around the poles. That way you won't unbalance your horse when he's doing all those flying lead changes."

Stevie looked puzzled.

"Look." Sal pointed to the middle of the arena. "Just pretend there are about six poles lined up over there and watch what I do."

The girls watched as Sal turned Sadie straight down the middle of the arena. "Okay," she called. "Somebody say go and I'll pretend I'm pole bending."

"Go!" said Carole.

Suddenly Sadie leaped forward at a full gallop. Twenty feet later she made a quick curve to the right; twenty feet after that, a quick curve to the left. San Antonio Sal was weaving through a pole bending course without a pole in

30

sight. At the end of the arena, Sadie made a sharp half turn and they zigzagged back up to the girls.

"Wheee!" Sal let go of her reins and lifted her arms high above her head as she and Sadie roared past them. "I won!"

"Wow!" said Lisa. "That was incredible!"

"Oh, well, it wasn't much." Sal rode back around and looked at Stevie. "Did you see what I meant, though, about leaning back when your horse makes his turn? They're twisting and lead changing so hard and fast they appreciate anything you can do to keep them balanced."

"Gosh," Stevie said. "Thanks. Now at least I'll know what I'm supposed to do."

"Hey, I was going to ask you girls if you wanted to ride out in the country with me and Sadie. I haven't been up here in years, and I'd kind of like to see how the landscape's changed."

"Sure," said Carole. "I'd love to go."

"Me too." Lisa gave Ghost a pat. "Stevie? How about you?"

"Oh, I think I'll stay here and work on my pole bending. If Gabriel was out here practicing, then I feel like that's what I'd better be doing, too. You guys go on ahead. I'll do a trail ride later."

"Are you sure?" Carole frowned. Normally Stevie was the first one to suggest a trail ride.

"Sure I'm sure. Tumbleweed and I will stay here and practice our flying lead changes."

31

"Okay." Carole and Pogo trotted after the others. "See you later."

Stevie watched as her friends rode out of the arena. As much as she wanted to go with them, the only thing she could think about right then was Gabriel, and the whole idea of him made her mad. *How could someone so obnoxious and annoying grab so much of my attention?* she asked herself. Maybe it was because they'd lived so close together these past few days. *Maybe whoever you live close to could just take over your brain, and I just had the bad luck to get stuck with Gabriel.* She pulled a knot out of Tumbleweed's mane and frowned. *But if obnoxious Gabriel's taken over my mind, then who's taken over Phil's? What if there's a girl he's living close to who's smart and funny and likes the outdoors? Somebody like that could really take over someone's brain!* Stevie shook her head. She couldn't allow herself to think about that right then. She had twenty-four hours to get ready for five different rodeo events.

"Come on, Tumbleweed," she said. She clucked to the horse and headed toward the spot where Sal had given her demonstration. "We need to bend some imaginary poles, and we need to bend them fast!"

32

4

BY THE TIME Shelly Bean clanged the triangle for lunch, Stevie had finished her first practice with Tumbleweed. She cooled him down and returned him to his stall, then hurried back to the wagon train to eat with her friends. She found Lisa and Carole sitting under a tree, just finishing their lunch of stewed apples and potato pancakes.

"Grab a plate, Stevie, and join us," Lisa called, looking up from the notebook she was writing in.

Stevie hurried through the chow line and sat down just as her friends were filling in some details of the journal they were keeping for Deborah.

"You and Tumbleweed must have had quite a practice," said Carole, noticing Stevie's sweaty face.

"We did," replied Stevie as she took her first bite of pancake. "He's a great little horse." She grinned. "And I just know he's a whole lot faster than Napoleon."

Carole and Lisa glanced at each other. They were growing tired of Stevie's obsession with Gabriel, and neither wanted to spoil their lunch break by discussing it. "You know, we need to write some things about San Antonio Sal in here," Lisa said. "She's the first rodeo clown I've ever met."

"Me too," said Carole. "Write down all that stuff she told us about clowning—about how each clown has her own clown personality and each of them can do special tricks."

Lisa nodded as she made notes. "And all of them have to entertain the audience as well as help the riders get out of the ring safely. It must be hard work.

"San Antonio Sal's so funny," Lisa continued. "I can't wait to meet the Texarkana Twins. They must really be a hoot."

"I know." Carole giggled. "Remember all those jokes she told us about rodeo cowboys?"

Lisa nodded with a grin. Both girls waited for Stevie, who loved jokes above all else, to ask to hear one, but she remained silent, just picking at her lunch and gazing over at the rodeo arena.

"Hello?" Carole reached over and tapped Stevie on her knee. "Carole to Stevie. Joke alert! You're about to miss some good ones!"

"Huh?" Stevie looked up as if she hadn't heard a word they'd said.

"Stevie, you've got to get a grip on this!" Lisa cried. "Gabriel is just one know-it-all, arrogant guy. You're letting this competition with him take over your life!"

Stevie blinked. "Gabriel?"

"Yes. Gabriel," said Carole. "He's all you've thought about since you two made that silly bet."

"No, he's not." Stevie shook her head. "I wasn't thinking about him at all just then."

"All right, then what were you thinking about?" asked Lisa. "What has got you so deep in thought that you didn't even hear someone talking about some terrific jokes they just heard?"

"Oh, it's not important." Embarrassed, Stevie looked down at her plate.

Carole frowned again. "Of course it's important, Stevie, if it's zoning you out to Mars. Just tell us what it is. Remember, we're The Saddle Club. We're duty bound to help."

Stevie blinked at her last bite of apple. "I was just thinking about Phil," she finally admitted with a sigh.

"Phil?" Carole and Lisa looked at each other in astonishment. "What about Phil?"

Stevie sighed. "Oh, just that ever since I've been stuck here with that twerp Gabriel, Phil's probably been rafting down the river with some pretty neat girl. I bet he's met

35

someone who's prettier than me and smarter than me and more fun than me," she said miserably.

"Oh, Stevie, that's just not possible," said Lisa. "Phil likes you more than anybody. You two make a perfect couple."

"We did until we took these separate vacations. Now every night he's probably dreaming about some cute girl on his raft who looks terrific in a swimsuit and paddles like a pro!"

"Stevie, I don't think Phil would fall head over heels in love with a totally new person that fast," reasoned Carole. "After all, his days must be pretty busy, too, if he's navigating a white-water river and camping in a different place every night. He's probably too tired to even think about anything romantic!"

"I don't know," Stevie muttered, remembering her own unwelcome dreams about Gabriel. "Phil's got a lot of energy."

"Did I overhear someone talking about energy?"

The girls looked over their shoulders. Gabriel stood there grinning, his cowboy hat pushed back on his head at a rakish angle.

"Actually, you were overhearing a private conversation," Lisa told him stiffly.

"Sorry," he said. "I didn't mean to intrude. I just saw Stevie practicing her pole bending and wondered how Tumbleweed was working out for her."

"Fine," answered Stevie, turning to face him. "He's a great horse. One of the fastest I've ever ridden."

Gabriel laughed. "That may be, but he looks like a real nag next to Napoleon."

Stevie narrowed her eyes. "You know, a horse is only half the team. You've got to be a darn good rider to know how to use one."

"Absolutely," Gabriel agreed. "Particularly in calf roping. I was the junior county champion calf roper in my state last year."

"Oh, really?" said Stevie. "I was the junior champion barrel racer of the Bar None riders last year."

"That's pretty good, for a girly sport like barrel racing," Gabriel said. "Are you any good at goat wrestling?"

Stevie tossed her head. "Of course I'm good at goat wrestling. I can pin a goat to the ground in eight seconds flat."

"Oh?" Gabriel raised one eyebrow. "Would you like to bet on that?"

"Sure," Stevie replied. "What'll it be?"

Lisa and Carole looked at each other in horror. To their knowledge, Stevie had never touched a goat, let alone wrestled one, in her life.

Gabriel spoke quickly. "Let's say that if you pin a goat in eight seconds flat, you get to make me perform any dare of your choice. If you can't, then I get to make you do any dare of my choice."

37

"Oh, make it more interesting than that," said Stevie, faking a yawn.

"Okay." Gabriel leaned back and stuck his thumbs in the belt loops of his jeans. "How about, whoever does better in the whole rodeo gets to make the loser perform one super dare of their choice? All five events. No holds barred, no questions asked."

"You're on!" Stevie leaped to her feet and again stuck out her hand. "Shake on it!"

"So much for trying to get her interested in rodeo clowns!" Lisa whispered to Carole as Gabriel and Stevie shook hands.

After they had sealed their wager, Gabriel tipped his hat to the girls and strolled whistling toward the arena.

"Why are you two looking at me like that?" Stevie asked when she turned back to her friends.

"Stevie, how many goats have you wrestled in your life?" Carole asked.

"Well, none," Stevie confessed. "I fudged a little on that one. But how hard can it be? I've wrestled my brothers, and they all smell like goats."

"And how many calves have you roped and poles have you bent, Miss Champion Barrel Racer of the Bar None Riders?" Lisa questioned her further.

"Not too many," admitted Stevie.

"Almost none," corrected Carole. "And you weren't the champion barrel racer of the Bar None Ranch, either. Kate was!"

"Okay, so I stretched the truth a little."

Carole frowned. "Stevie, I'm getting really worried about you."

"Why?" Stevie looked puzzled.

"Because you haven't been this competitive in a long time, and it seems to be taking over every moment of your life. You're bragging about things that aren't true, and you're not even enjoying our trip anymore because of this competition." Carole shook her head. "Plus, who knows what a jerk like Gabriel might make you do if he wins the bet?"

"Yeah," agreed Lisa. "It might be something really humiliating!"

"But you two are assuming he's going to win," Stevie replied. "He's not. I am. Don't worry about what he might make me do. Help me think up some appropriately disgusting thing I can make him do!"

"I don't know, Stevie." Carole frowned. "He's had a lot more experience at these rodeo events than you."

"Yoo-hoo! Girls!" Another voice rang out. "I've been looking all over the place for you three!"

The girls turned again. San Antonio Sal was hurrying up to their spot beneath the tree, clutching a sheet of white paper.

"I'm so glad I found you!" she said breathlessly. "I've got a real emergency on my hands!"

"What's wrong?" Lisa asked quickly.

Sal waved the sheet of paper at the girls. "This is a

message the lady down at the rodeo office took for me. The Texarkana Twins just called from Donnersville. They ate a whole mess of bad catfish last night and came down with food poisoning. They're not going to be able to make the rodeo!"

"Oh no!" cried Carole. "We really wanted to meet them."

"Well, that's not the worst part. All sanctioned rodeo events must have a team of three clowns. I've called every clown within two hundred miles and they're all booked for bigger rodeos. If I can't find two replacements by tomorrow, the junior events will have to be canceled!"

"That's terrible!" Lisa exclaimed.

"Well, that's where I was wondering if maybe you girls could help me out. I've seen how well all three of you ride, and you seem to have a lot of good old-fashioned cow sense about you. Would you be willing to take over the Texarkana Twins' part of the act? I could show you the routines and teach you how to do the makeup. Plus, we'll be working the junior events, so you won't be contending with any wild broncs or bulls." Sal smiled hopefully. "Course, it will mean you won't be able to compete, since you'll be working the whole time."

"Count me in!" cried Carole. "I can ride in a junior rodeo some other time, but I'll probably never get the chance to be a rodeo clown again!"

"Me too," said Lisa. "Especially if without us, the junior events will be canceled."

Everyone looked at Stevie, waiting for her to join them. "I don't know," she finally mumbled, frowning.

"Stevie, how can you not say yes?" Lisa asked. "It's what The Saddle Club is supposed to do! Help out at all times!"

"I know," said Stevie. "And if you and Carole weren't here I'd certainly do it. But since you two are here and you're such good riders, you really don't need me." She took a deep breath and looked at San Antonio Sal. "I hope you'll understand, but I'd rather compete in the events this time. I know Carole and Lisa will do a great job helping you out."

Carole's and Lisa's faces fell, but San Antonio Sal gave Stevie a big wink.

"That's okay, Stevie. I understand. I think you've got something to prove tomorrow, and with the help of your friends here, you'll still have the opportunity to prove it."

Sal turned to Carole and Lisa. "Okay, girls. My trailer's parked beneath the west grandstand. After you finish your lunch, come on down there and we'll get to work. By tomorrow afternoon you two will be real live rodeo clowns!"

"WHY, HELLO THERE, Stevie," Pete Parsons called as Stevie walked into the cool dimness of the Rocking S stable. "I thought you were done riding for the day."

She looked around. Pete sat on a bale of hay, twirling a small lasso in a crazy-looking circle.

Stevie smiled and shook her head. "No, Pete, I'm nowhere near done for the day. In fact, I think I probably should have skipped lunch and just stayed on Tumbleweed."

Pete effortlessly spun the lasso out in a wide figure eight. "How so? Did you get so tired of driving that old Conestoga wagon that now you're hankering to spend all day in the saddle?"

"No. It's a lot more serious than that."

"What do you mean?" Pete quit spinning the rope and looked at her.

Stevie told him the story of Gabriel and his superior attitude and how he thought he was a much better rider than she was and how they had a bet going to settle it once and for all.

"You know, I wondered if that boy wasn't acting a little too big for his britches when he first came in here." Pete frowned and stroked his thick black mustache. "But I watched you on Tumbleweed. You're a good enough rider to beat him."

"I know I can beat him in the quarter-mile race and the barrel racing," said Stevie. "But I have my doubts about those other events."

"Oh, you're probably just a little rusty. It'll all come back to you when the chutes open."

Stevie shook her head. "No, Pete, you don't understand. I only learned how to pole bend this morning, and I've never roped a calf in a rodeo or wrestled a goat in my life!"

Pete's brown eyes widened. "You've never roped any calves? Nor wrestled one goat in your entire life?" He moved the piece of straw he was chewing from one corner of his mouth to the other and frowned at Stevie.

"I've never roped in a competition, and I haven't done any roping at all in a while," Stevie answered honestly.

"Well," he said, gathering up his rope and unfolding

43

himself from the bale of hay, "that's a horse of a different color. I guess we'd better get busy. You need some emergency rodeo training, and you need it pronto!"

"WOW!" CAROLE BREATHED as she and Lisa stepped inside San Antonio Sal's trailer. "This is the most fabulous place I've ever seen!"

The girls looked around the small, colorful room. Every inch was covered with clown equipment. The floor was lined with all sorts of purple and green wigs on stands, and boxes overflowed with polka-dot parasols, water-squirting flowers, and rubber chickens. A large, brightly lit mirror hung on one wall between two clothes racks, where baggy, oversized pants dangled next to sequined vests and crazy tie-dyed blouses.

Lisa blinked at the bright, glittery colors. "I've never seen so many spangles and sparkles and sequins in my life!"

"Well, it ain't much, but it's home." San Antonio Sal chuckled. "Y'all sit down here and we'll get to work."

The girls sat down in front of the mirror. Sal pulled out one huge makeup kit full of greasepaint and charcoal pencils, then another one with fake noses and floppy false ears and fuzzy stick-on eyebrows.

"Let's invent your personalities first," she said, uncapping a tube of clear face cream. "Then you'll know what kind of clown to be."

"What do you mean?" Carole asked.

"Well, if you draw on a sad face, then your clown moves are going to be slower and your body language will be more droopy." Sal squirted out some cream for Lisa. "If you put on a goofy face, then you'll clown in a looser, less controlled way."

"Oh, I think I'll be goofy," giggled Lisa, rubbing the cream onto her face. "I'd never get the chance to do that at home."

"What if you just want to be happy?" Carole asked Sal.

"Happy's probably the best face to put on," Sal said. "That way you can be anything—mad, sad, goofy—according to what goes on in the ring."

"What are you?" asked Lisa.

"I'm always happy," answered Sal. "Texarkana Cindy's usually goofy, while Texarkana Ruth's usually mad. It works out pretty well for us in the ring."

"Wow." Lisa looked at all the tubes of greasepaint scattered in front of Sal's mirror. "There are so many possibilities."

Sal laughed. "That's what makes clowning such a wonderful life. Every day you can be somebody different, and every day you get to make people laugh. Sometimes you even get to save a cowboy's life." She rummaged through a drawer under the table and pulled out a book. "Here's an album of clown face designs. Look through there and maybe you can get some ideas."

Carole giggled as she and Lisa turned the pages of the

45

clown book. "I wonder if Stevie's having this much fun," she whispered.

"TWIRL, TWIRL, TWIRL, TWIRL, throw!" Stevie said to herself as she swung the lasso. She was practicing her cattle roping at a target Pete had rigged up for her—a plastic calf's head stuck in a bale of hay. She swung the lasso one final time, then let it go. The loop soared through the air, only to fall harmlessly to the ground a foot away from the plastic head.

"Darn!" she said, dismounting for the twentieth time. "This isn't working and I'm doing everything just like I'm supposed to!"

Disgustedly she re-coiled the lasso and walked back to Tumbleweed. There was a sympathetic look in the horse's eyes, as if he wished he could do something to help her. She rubbed his neck. "Maybe we should take a break," she said. "My right arm feels like it's on fire from all this roping."

She grabbed Tumbleweed's reins and led him to a tall cottonwood tree that grew at one end of the corral. For the past three hours she had practiced what Pete had shown her—everything from tightening the noose of a rope to fit over a calf's head to learning how to lean low in the saddle before she started to tackle a goat. As nearly as she could tell, the only progress she had made was to irritate her aching hands and make her rear end even sorer than it had been when she was driving the wagon.

"I don't know, Tumbleweed," she said softly as the sturdy little horse took long swallows of water from the trough. "I've done this before, but I'm really out of practice. This time I might have seriously overestimated my talents as a cowgirl."

"Hi!" said a familiar voice behind her. She knew without looking that it was Gabriel.

"Hi," she answered, quickly rearranging her expression from dismay into confidence. She grinned broadly. "How's it going?"

"Great," he said, leaning against the top rail of the fence. He'd changed into a shirt that made his eyes look even bluer than they normally did. He nodded at the plastic calf's head protruding from the bale of hay and smiled. "Need a little practice, huh?"

Stevie shrugged. "I was just testing out Tumbleweed. I'm in great shape."

"I see," said Gabriel. He dangled one end of the rope he held in his hands and looked at the ground. "You know, I've been thinking about this bet we've got going."

"Oh?" Stevie's heart began to beat faster. Maybe Gabriel was about to chicken out.

"Yeah. In fact, I've been thinking about it all day."

Stevie smiled to herself. He was trying to find a way to weasel out of it! Maybe there was a chance they could forget this whole thing and she could get back to having some fun with Lisa and Carole. "And?" she asked hopefully.

47

"And I've just decided what I'm going to make you do when I win!" he announced gleefully.

"When you *win?*" she repeated as she felt her face heat up with both anger and disappointment.

"Yeah. When I win." He looked at her and smiled. "It's really going to be great! Everybody's going to love it!"

"Oh, really? What is it?" Stevie asked in spite of herself.

"Are you kidding?" He laughed and tilted his hat back on his head. "Do you honestly think I'd tell you beforehand? Forget it! That's for me to know and you to find out!"

"Well, before you start enjoying your little dare too much, you'd better start worrying about what I'm going to make you do when *I* win," retorted Stevie quickly. "It'll go down in the annals of rodeo history! And I'm not telling you, either!"

"Fine!" said Gabriel.

"Fine!" Stevie cried back, watching with clenched fists as he slung his rope over his shoulder and sauntered off toward the stable. She snorted. Gabriel was undoubtedly the most impossible person she'd ever met, and now she was involved in a bet with him she couldn't get out of!

"Come on, Tumbleweed," she said, leading the horse back to the plastic calf head after Gabriel was out of sight. "Now not only do we have to win, we have to think up some totally disgusting thing for him to do!" She looked

48

at the horse and gave a grim smile. "But we'll do it, even if we have to practice all night!"

IN THE RODEO arena, three clowns were rolling out a dented barrel. One clown was tall, with bright red hair and a sequined vest. The other two were shorter. One wore a baggy black suit and a derby along with a red nose and candy-striped socks, while the other sported a frizzy green wig with pointed Martian ears and an old-timey long-sleeved purple bathing suit.

"I must say, y'all look just as good as the Texarkana Twins," Sal laughed as Lisa and Carole helped her maneuver the barrel out into the arena.

"Well, I feel pretty happy." Carole laughed and pulled up one of her striped socks.

"And I certainly feel goofy." Lisa adjusted the green wig on her head.

"Great. Just keep those feelings in mind while I show you our routines. That way everything will go perfectly."

Sal stood the barrel up on one end. It was lightweight but deep enough for a person to squeeze inside. "Let me give you a brief course in rodeo clowning. If you've ever noticed before, rodeo clowns usually work in teams of three. We have a bullfighter, a point clown, and a barrel man. The bullfighter is a clown who jumps around and tries to distract the bull after the rider's off his back. You have to be nimble and quick to be a bullfighter."

"And brave, too," added Carole.

"Absolutely," Sal agreed. She thumped the barrel. "The barrel man stays inside here and watches the bullfighter work. If the bullfighter is having trouble with a bull, he leads him over to the barrel man, who stands up inside the barrel and draws the bull over to him. Then the barrel man scrunches down inside in case the bull decides the barrel would make good target practice for his horns." Sal laughed and pointed to a large dent on one side of her barrel. "That was put there by a bull named Percy who just didn't like the color of my wig one day."

"What does the point clown do?" asked Lisa.

"The point clown coordinates everybody else. If she sees the bullfighter needs help, she goes there; if the barrel man's getting tossed around too much, she helps out there. If everything's going okay, the point clown entertains the audience."

"That sounds like the toughest job of all," said Carole.

"Oh, they're all tough in their own ways, but they're also a lot of fun." Sal noticed Lisa's wary expression. "Anyway, we'll be working the junior events, so we won't have any broncs or bulls to worry about. Just calves and goats." She laughed. "They're not real strong, but they can be slippery little devils."

She banged on the barrel. "Okay. Who wants to be the barrel man? Or should I say barrel girl?"

Lisa shrugged. "I'll give it a try."

"Great," Sal said. "Hop right in there and Carole and I

will roll you around the arena. We can work on our routines as we go along."

Lisa squirmed down into the barrel.

"Are you ready?" said Sal.

"Ready!" called Lisa.

"Okay, then, clowns. Let's go!"

AS THE PURPLE evening shadows grew long over the corral, Stevie's lasso finally fell exactly over the calf's head.

"All right!" she cried as she wearily climbed off Tumbleweed. "After about a hundred throws, I finally got him!" She sighed as she loosened the rope from the plastic head. It was getting too dark to practice anymore, and she knew she was still far from good.

"Okay," she said to herself. "I may not win the calf roping, but if I'm lucky, at least I won't totally disgrace myself." She re-coiled the rope, then started to walk Tumbleweed back to the barn. The setting sun turned the filmy clouds a brilliant shade of orange.

"I wonder if Phil is having as pretty a sunset as we are?" Stevie asked aloud as Tumbleweed clopped along behind her. "I wonder if he's toasting marshmallows around a campfire or strumming a guitar or skipping rocks across a river?" She felt a sharp pang in her stomach as she imagined Phil with a new girl by his side. She would enjoy doing all the things Phil liked to do, and they would be sitting side by side every day, telling each other jokes, holding hands when the river was calm and paddling furiously through the rapids together, all the while gazing into each other's eyes.

"And here I am, alone in the middle of a dusty corral, throwing a rope around a plastic calf head," Stevie moaned. "I'm dirty and I'm sore and now I'll probably lose the rodeo tomorrow and then I'll have to do some stupid, humiliating thing that Gabriel dreamed up!

"Oh, Tumbleweed," she sighed, reaching up to rub the horse behind one of his soft ears. "How do I get into such messes?"

6

"THIS IS THE first soft thing we've sat on in over a week!" Lisa exclaimed, nestling into the old movie theater seat. "It almost seems like we're back in civilization again."

"I know," Carole said. "Feels good, doesn't it?"

"It sure does." Lisa laughed. "Particularly after spending most of the afternoon rolling around in a barrel. I feel like I've been launched into outer space!"

The girls were attending, along with all the other pioneers, a prerodeo talent show put on by the people of Clinchport. An old theater on the town square had been made into an auditorium, and the seats were filling up fast. When the houselights blinked three times, everyone realized the show was about to start.

"But you've got to admit clowning was fun," Carole

53

said. "I mean, putting on all that crazy makeup and then learning how to do those tricks with the horses. This was one of the neatest days I've ever had!"

Lisa and Carole giggled, then turned to Stevie. "How did your day go, Stevie?" Lisa asked. "We saw you practicing hard for the goat wrestling when we went to get Sal's bull barrel."

"Huh?" Stevie turned her gaze away from the hay bales that decorated each corner of the old stage and looked at her friends.

"I said, how did your day go?" Lisa repeated.

"Oh, great." Stevie rubbed her right shoulder as if it were sore. "After I practiced what San Antonio Sal told me about pole bending, Pete from the stable helped me with the other events. I worked on my dismounts in goat wrestling for most of the afternoon. Then I finished up by perfecting my lasso release for calf roping."

"Gosh, Stevie," said Carole. "That sounds like something my dad would dream up for his new Marine recruits. You should have joined us and had some fun learning how to clown."

"Yeah." Lisa looked at Stevie with concern. "It doesn't sound like you had nearly as much fun as we did."

"Oh, I'll have my fun tomorrow," Stevie promised with a wicked grin, "when I win the rodeo and that creep Gabriel has to do the dare of my choice." She frowned. "What do you think of making him put on my old pioneer dress and do 'women's work' for a day?"

Carole laughed. "For Gabriel, I think that would be a fate worse than death!"

"Hi, girls," someone called. They looked toward the stage. Bouncing on the seat in front of them was Eileen, her blond ponytail flying in the air with every bounce.

"You'd better stop, Eileen," Lisa warned. "You're going to break that seat."

"You can't make me!" retorted Eileen. "Nobody can make me do anything!"

"Probably not," Carole agreed with a sigh. She turned back to Stevie and Lisa. "Anyway, Stevie, guess what we learned to do with the horses today—"

"I know a secret!" Eileen blurted out in a singsongy voice.

Stevie and Lisa ignored her as Carole told about the fun they'd had learning Sal's fall-asleep-on-your-horse routine.

"I said, I know a secret!" Eileen jumped harder on the seat and singsonged even more loudly.

"Okay, Eileen." Stevie frowned at her. "So you know a secret. Good for you."

"No, I know a really *big* secret!" Eileen insisted. "One that you probably would just love to know yourself!"

Just as Stevie was about to tell Eileen to sit down and be quiet, the houselights dimmed. "Ladies and gentlemen," a voice announced over a loudspeaker. "The people of Clinchport proudly present the Clinchport High School Drill Team!"

The red velvet curtains opened. Three rows of high-school girls marched onto the stage. Some carried white rifles on their shoulders, while others waved American flags. They marched around the stage in a close-order drill to a recording of "Stars and Stripes Forever." Everyone began to clap in time to the music, and for once Eileen had to be quiet.

Three hours later the talent show was over and the girls slowly walked back to their wagon.

"That was fun, wasn't it?" said Lisa. "Those cowboys who yodeled were terrific."

Carole nodded and laughed. "They were. And I really loved the guy who danced with the pig."

"Wasn't he cool?" Stevie giggled in agreement. "That would be a terrific thing for me to make Gabriel do."

"Stevie, did you sit through that whole show just thinking about what hideous dare you could dream up for Gabriel?" Carole asked.

"Well, not the whole show," said Stevie. "Just a few parts of it. And they gave me some wonderful ideas!"

The girls got back to their wagon and pulled their sleeping bags out into the cool night air. Carole found a soft patch of ground under a tree, and soon all three of them had snuggled down for the night.

"Good night, everybody," yawned Lisa.

"Good night, Texarkana Lisa," Carole replied. "Good night, Stevie, queen of the rodeo."

"Good night, you guys."

Stevie rolled over on her side and fell into a deep sleep. At first she did not dream at all; then she began to have weird visions of horses and goats and dancing pigs. At one point Carole and Lisa floated across her dream sky in their clown costumes, while in another dream her brother Chad kept holding up a valentine heart and laughing at her. In her longest dream she and Phil were out in the desert on horseback. They were getting ready to run a quarter-mile race. San Antonio Sal stood at the starting line with a pistol in her hand, while Gabriel waited by the finish line on Stevie's side of the track.

Across from Gabriel stood a girl with beautiful green eyes and golden-red hair, smiling and waving at Phil. Phil blew her a kiss, then turned to Stevie. "That's Meghan," he said dreamily. "She speaks fluent Italian, she won a full scholarship to Harvard when she was in the sixth grade, and she plays polo." Phil smiled and patted his horse's neck. "She even loaned me her horse to ride." Stevie looked down at Phil's horse. It was a huge bay stallion that tossed his head and snorted fire. Stevie saw the name *Secretariat* stitched on his red sequined saddle pad.

"Meghan owns Secretariat?" Stevie heard her own voice come out in a mousy squeak. Phil grinned and nodded. "She's rich, too."

"Uh-huh." Stevie blinked and looked down at her mount. It was not Tumbleweed she was on, or her own

57

horse, Belle. Stevie was getting ready for a race against Secretariat on Nero, the oldest, most decrepit gelding in Pine Hollow!

"Wait!" she cried, her words seeming to come out in slow motion. "That's not fair! You can't expect Nero to keep up with Secretariat!"

Phil shrugged. Then it was too late. San Antonio Sal fired the starting gun, and Phil and the big bay stallion bounded off in a cloud of dust.

"No!" Stevie cried. "Wait! It's not fair!"

She sat up and opened her eyes, fully expecting to see Phil and Secretariat disappearing before her. Instead she saw Mr. Cate, struggling to get his water bucket back inside his wagon.

"I'm sorry if we woke you up!" he called in a hoarse whisper. He started to laugh. "Mrs. Cate kicked the bucket in her sleep and knocked it out of the wagon!"

"It's okay," Stevie whispered back, grateful to have been awakened from her nightmare. "It didn't bother me a bit."

Stevie tried to catch her breath as Mr. Cate climbed back inside his wagon. She rubbed her eyes and looked up at the million twinkling stars overhead. Though she knew a part of her was being crazy and irrational about Phil and his new girlfriend, it seemed as if that part was taking over the other, more normal parts of her. Not only did she worry about them during the day, but now they were showing up in her dreams at night!

Maybe this is some kind of ESP, she thought with alarm as she gazed up at the stars. *Maybe my dreams are trying to prepare me for the worst. Maybe there really is a girl with golden-red hair whom Phil has fallen in love with!*

She sat up straighter and shook her head. *You have no proof of that*, she lectured herself firmly. *You don't even know if any girls are on Phil's trip in the first place. And if there are any, you don't know that they're cute. And you certainly don't know that Phil has fallen in love with any of them. All you have is a bunch of feelings and dreams and worries.*

She looked over at Lisa and Carole, who were sleeping soundly, then settled back down in her sleeping bag. "Even if he has fallen in love with some wonderful red-headed girl, there's nothing I can do about it tonight," she sighed. "The best thing for me to do right now is to try to get some sleep. There's a big rodeo tomorrow, and I've got to win it!"

7

"I CAN'T FIND MY green wig!" Lisa cried. She stood in the middle of the wagon dressed in her long purple bathing suit, a puzzled expression on her face.

"Look outside, in that plastic storage box Sal gave us," said Carole, who was pulling up her red-and-white-striped socks.

"Good idea."

"But watch out for Stevie's lasso," Carole called as Lisa jumped out of the wagon. "She's practicing her releases."

Suddenly Carole heard a shriek and a thud. She scrambled to the open end of the wagon and looked out. Lisa sat on the ground, a tangle of rope draped around her arms and shoulders.

"Lisa! Are you okay?" Stevie hurried over to her friend.

"I'm so sorry! I was aiming at the bucket on the back of the wagon! I'd just thrown the rope when you came out!"

"I'm okay," Lisa said as Stevie untangled the rope from around her. "Just as long as you didn't mistake me for a cow!"

Stevie laughed and helped Lisa to her feet. "I don't know too many cows that come to the rodeo dressed in purple long johns!"

"Is everyone all right?" Carole asked.

"We're fine," Stevie and Lisa replied.

"I saw what you did to her!" a smaller voice called. Eileen stood beside the wagon, dressed in her pioneer costume, her hair now in pigtails.

"Oh, buzz off, Eileen," said Lisa as she began to rummage in the big plastic box for her wig. "Stevie didn't do anything to me. It was an accident."

"You don't know that for sure," Eileen snapped back.

"Hey, Eileen, why aren't you dressed for the rodeo?" Stevie asked as she re-coiled her rope. "I thought you were doing some bull riding today."

"Not me!" cried Eileen, her green eyes wide. "I would never do anything that dirty and dusty and dangerous!" She watched Stevie as she began to twirl her rope again. "Anyway, I know a secret that's a lot more fun than riding any stupid bull!"

"Really?" Stevie aimed her lasso at the wagon wheel. The noose fell around it cleanly on the first try. Stevie pulled the rope taut, then gathered it up and started all over again.

Eileen smiled coyly. "Yes. It's about two people you know really well."

"You don't say?" This time Stevie turned her attention to the parking brake at the front of the wagon. She made the noose smaller, then twirled the lasso over her head and let go. Again the noose hit its target dead on.

"Yes," Eileen said smugly. "And one of them has blue eyes."

"No kidding?" Stevie walked to the parking brake and loosened her rope. "Gosh, I wonder how many blue-eyed people might be on this wagon train. Ten? Twenty?" She turned and studied Eileen for a long moment. Slowly she started to twirl the rope again. "You know what we do with people who keep secrets around here?" she asked with a menacing grin.

"What?" Eileen stuck out her chest and tried to look fearless.

"We rope 'em." Stevie raised the lariat over her head and twirled it faster and faster. "And then we hog-tie 'em and hitch 'em to the back of the wagon and let Yankee and Doodle pull 'em around the camp until they beg for mercy!"

"No-o-o-o!" Eileen gave a thin little scream and ran off toward her parents' campsite.

"What was that noise?" Carole jumped out of the wagon, dressed in her clown costume.

Stevie chuckled. "That was the sound of a terrified Eileen."

"What happened? Did she lose her teddy bear again?" Carole asked with a frown.

"No," Stevie replied. "She was running away so that I wouldn't rope and hog-tie her and let the horses drag her around the camp."

"Stevie, did you say something to upset the poor little dear?" Carole could barely contain a laugh.

"Well, maybe a little something," Stevie admitted. Then she remembered all the trouble Eileen had caused everyone in general and herself in particular. "But it was nothing she didn't deserve," she added.

"Hey, Carole, are you ready to go?" Lisa asked, finally pulling the green wig out of the box and fitting it on her head. "Since we're going to have to put on our faces in Sal's trailer, we should get a move on."

"I'm ready." Carole adjusted her derby to just the right angle and gave her candy-striped hose a final tug. "Stevie, are you coming with us?"

"You two go ahead," said Stevie. "I'm going to practice my roping a little longer. I'll catch up with you at the arena before everything begins."

"Okay," said Carole as she and Lisa began to walk toward the rodeo grounds. "We'll see you later."

Stevie smiled as she watched the purple clown with green hair and the baggy-suited clown in a derby run down the grassy hillside. Then she went back inside the wagon and pulled out her journal. She and Phil were each keeping a diary of their trip to share when they got home, but she'd been too busy to write anything in hers since she'd been practicing for the rodeo. Now she wanted to jot down all the details of the past two days before she forgot them. Hurriedly she scribbled about the bet she'd made with Gabriel, how hard she'd been practicing for the rodeo, and how Lisa and Carole were learning to be clowns. *They are having a lot of fun*, she wrote, then looked up from her paper.

"I wonder what Phil's writing in his journal," she said aloud. She frowned, remembering her dream about Secretariat and Phil and the girl with golden-red hair. "He's probably writing about rafting down some river with this beautiful girl. She's whispering in his ear in Italian, and he's probably asked her to be his date for the big Halloween dance at school next fall." Tears began to fill Stevie's eyes. She looked at the lariat curled in one corner of the wagon. "Oh, stop it, you nitwit!" she chided herself. "Pull yourself together! You don't know that any of that's true, and besides, you've got a rodeo to win today!" With that, she put her journal away and jumped out of the wagon, determined to practice her roping even harder than before.

The rodeo started at midmorning. The day was perfect—white clouds floated high in a deep blue sky and the sunshine sparkled with a gentle warmth. A portable fence divided the arena in two, with the adult events taking place in one half and the junior events in the other. Stevie and Carole and Lisa stood by the fence watching as a four-person color guard rode out on gorgeous paint horses and paraded the American flag around the adult side of the arena. Everyone stood at attention as the Clinchport High School Band played the national anthem.

"Pretty neat, huh?" Carole's eyes glowed with pride as she held her derby over her heart.

"Always is." Stevie smiled, replacing her cowboy hat on her head after the band had finished. "Here," she said, handing Carole and Lisa two safety pins and a sheet of paper with the number 33 in big black letters. "Would you pin this on my back?"

"Sure." Carole held the paper while Lisa pinned it straight across Stevie's shoulders. "I'm glad you got thirty-three, Stevie. It feels like a real lucky number."

"Do you think so?" Stevie twisted around and tried to read her back. "Gabriel's got number seven."

"Oh, thirty-three's a whole lot luckier than seven," Lisa assured her.

"It better be," Stevie said grimly with a flinty, determined look in her eyes.

"Hey, Stevie. Relax!" Carole grinned and wiggled her red rubber nose. "This may be a competition, but don't forget it's still supposed to be fun!"

"I know." Stevie walked in a little circle and began to twirl her lariat nervously. "I just wish they would go ahead and start."

"Ladies and gentlemen," the ring announcer called a moment later. "Welcome to Clinchport's Pioneer Days Rodeo! The first events of the day will be barrel racing for the juniors and bronc riding for the adults. All riders, take your places now!"

"Good luck, Stevie!" Lisa and Carole each gave Stevie a quick hug. "We'll see you in the ring."

"Thanks!" Stevie said as she hurried off to join the other contestants. "I'll need it!"

San Antonio Sal walked out into the center of the ring and waved for Lisa and Carole to join her. As they had discussed the day before, they would clown the first event on foot, since no bucking calves or slippery goats would need to be caught.

"Are y'all feeling funny?" Sal asked as they trotted out to meet her.

"We sure are," Carole said, looking at the three barrels placed in a big triangle in the middle of the ring. It was around these barrels that Stevie would soon be racing.

"And how's our cowgirl Stevie doing?" Sal's red painted-on eyebrows wrinkled in concern.

"She's nervous," said Lisa. "But she's determined to win, and she's a pretty good barrel racer."

"Good for her." Sal grinned. "All right, Texarkana Lisa

and Texarkana Carole, if y'all are ready, then let's rock and roll!"

The girls followed Sal over to the sidelines, where they began their first routine—one where Sal and Carole fought over who got to push Lisa around in a baby carriage. Carole had just started the fight by bopping Sal over the head with a rubber bat when the ring announcer spoke.

"Our first junior barrel racer is Ms. Mary Corona from Arden Springs. Give her a big howdy, folks!"

Applause rippled through the crowd. The girls clowned through their routine while Mary Corona raced around the barrels. "If we keep an ear on the announcer, we can hear when Stevie's turn comes," Carole whispered as Lisa honked her big rubber nose.

"I know." Lisa winked back as Mary Corona crossed the finish line and the crowd laughed at their antics.

Clowning all the way, Sal and Carole pushed Lisa in the buggy down toward the middle of the arena. Over in the adult part of the rodeo, cowboys were trying to remain seated on bucking broncos while their crowd cheered. The other team of rodeo clowns and the pickup riders were working hard to see that all the cowboys got off their broncs and out of the arena safely.

"Wow," Lisa said as Sal stopped the baby carriage. "Looks like they're working a lot harder than we are."

"They are right now, but just wait till those goats come out," laughed Sal.

"Look!" Carole pointed to the far end of the arena. "Stevie's up next. I can see her at the starting line. And Gabriel's right after her!"

"Okay," Sal said. "I'll start juggling so y'all can watch, but remember not to cheer for her. We're clowns, and clowns root for everybody."

Sal started juggling three bowling pins while Carole and Lisa pretended to fight over the baby carriage. "Our next contestant is Ms. Stevie Lake," the announcer said. "All the way from Willow Creek, Virginia! Let's give this little Southern belle a big hand!"

The crowd cheered. All the pioneers from the wagon train were sitting together, so an especially loud chorus of whistles and cheers went up from them. Carole and Lisa looked at each other and rolled their eyes at the idea of Stevie's being a Southern belle. Then the starting buzzer sounded. They paused in their make-believe fight and held their breath as Stevie and Tumbleweed shot out of the chute. Stevie leaned into the first turn just as Jeannie and Eli had taught her at the Bar None Ranch; then they flew toward the second barrel. Tumbleweed's ears were slapped back as he galloped, and the girls could see a look of grim determination on Stevie's face. They twisted around the last barrel, then dashed toward the finish line. As they crossed it, a huge cheer went up from the crowd. Carole could see Mr. Cate standing up and whistling while Karen Nicely rang a cowbell.

"Whoa, Nellie!" the ring announcer cried. "That little

Southern belle can ride!" He paused, then continued, "Our next contestant is Gabriel Jackson, who's visiting us from Montana. Let her rip, Gabriel!"

Lisa and Carole watched as Gabriel and Napoleon took their place behind the starting line. When the buzzer sounded, the big palomino burst forward in a rush. He and Gabriel slid around the first barrel and raced to the second. They circled it cleanly. Gabriel leaned forward in the saddle and whacked Napoleon's rump as they circled the last barrel and rode hard toward the finish line. Again a cheer arose from the crowd as Gabriel pulled up in a cloud of dust.

"Nice job, young man," the ring announcer said. "That's all our barrel racing contestants, folks, and in just a moment we'll announce our results."

"What do you think?" Lisa asked Carole nervously.

"I don't know." Carole frowned. "They both looked awfully fast from this end of the arena."

They hurried back to where Sal was trying to juggle a tennis racket, a baseball bat, and a feather. The crowd roared with laughter as she got two things going but never all three together.

"How'd she do?" Sal whispered as the tennis racket came crashing to the ground at her feet.

"We don't know yet," said Carole. "They're figuring up the results."

"Well, we need to go get on our horses," Sal said. "Lisa, hop back in the baby carriage and we'll exit stage left."

Lisa sprawled comically in the buggy just as the ring announcer's voice rang out. "Ladies and gentlemen, today's champion junior barrel racer is our little Southern belle, Ms. Stevie Lake from Willow Creek, Virginia!"

Lisa started to clap but caught herself. "One down," she whispered happily to Carole as they rolled toward the exit. "Four to go!"

The next event was goat wrestling. It worked much like bulldogging, with the riders tackling goats, instead of calves, from horseback and pinning them to the ground. Though goats weighed less than calves, they were faster and a lot nimbler. Sal reminded the girls what their jobs were as they hurried over to their horses.

"Now, remember. Carole will act just like a hazer in calf roping and make sure the goat keeps running straight. Lisa, you'll make sure the rider's okay at all times, and I'll worry about making everything seem funny for the crowd."

"Where do we herd the goats after they've been pinned?" Carole asked as she made sure Pogo's cinch was tight.

Sal mounted Sadie and peered into the arena. "Head 'em over to that stock pen by the speaker's stand. The pickup boys want to save that big pen beside the racetrack for some of the nastier bulls the adults will ride."

"Okay," the girls said as they mounted up. They rode to the gate and waited as the grounds crew removed the barrels and set up the goat chute. Then they loped out onto the field, doing Sal's famous chase routine. By the time they had the crowd howling with laughter, the goat wrestling was ready to begin. Carole took her place on one side of the goat chute while Lisa rode over next to the riders' gate. Sal trotted down to the far end of the arena and began pulling balloons out of Sadie's left ear.

The first contestant was Mary Corona, the girl who had competed in barrel racing. She settled her horse down inside the gate, then gave a quick nod. The chute opened and a big white billy goat came charging out. Carole urged Pogo into a lope to keep up with him while Mary Corona burst out of her gate on a beautiful pinto mare. Lisa and Ghost followed slightly behind Mary as she chased the goat down one side of the arena. Mary leaned low over the goat's body, then grabbed his neck and slid off her horse. Though she pulled backward with all her strength, the goat managed to wiggle away from her. She chased him for a few steps, then lunged at his hind leg. He gave a small kick, then scurried away again as Mary Corona fell facedown in the dust. The buzzer sounded.

"Sorry, Mary, your time is up," the rodeo announcer said. "But give her a nice hand, anyway, folks. That was a good try."

Carole and Pogo herded the bleating goat over to the stock pen while Lisa reached down from Ghost and offered Mary a hand.

"Are you okay?" she asked.

"Yeah, I'm fine," the girl replied, dusting off her lacy

71

white cowboy shirt. "Just disappointed. This goat stuff is harder than it looks."

"Well, good luck in the next event," Lisa called as Mary walked back to the starting gate.

Carole returned, and they took their places again. The next three contestants had no luck at all. Carole and Lisa were beginning to wonder if anybody could successfully wrestle a goat when Gabriel's name was announced.

"Here's our young cowpoke from Montana again," the announcer said as Gabriel rode Napoleon into the starting gate. Carole and Lisa watched for the nod of his black cowboy hat. Then the chutes opened and his goat was off and running. Almost before Carole and Lisa could blink, Gabriel was off Napoleon and had the goat on his back, three of his legs tied with a bow. The crowd cheered.

"What a ride!" the announcer cried. "Tip your hat to the audience, young man! You're one heck of a goat-buster!"

Smiling, Gabriel took off his hat and waved to the audience. The girls watched as he remounted Napoleon and rode triumphantly around the ring.

"Watch out," Lisa whispered to Carole as they got back into position. "I think Stevie's next!"

"Our last contestant is Ms. Stevie Lake, from Virginia," the announcer said. "If she can wrestle a goat as well as she can circle a barrel, then all us Western cowboys are in trouble!"

Stevie and Tumbleweed settled down into the starting gate. Carole and Lisa both had butterflies in their stomachs as they watched a wrangler push a big black-and-white goat into the chute. They waited for Stevie's signal. The gates flew open.

The goat came out fast, but Tumbleweed was just as fast, running right alongside him. Stevie waited for an instant, choosing just the right moment, then leaned low over the goat and slid off Tumbleweed. She grabbed the goat by his neck and front leg, but she misjudged how fast he was running. Instead of pulling him down, Stevie rolled head over heels and pulled the goat upside down on top of her! Carole and Lisa could only watch helplessly while his four legs and Stevie's two legs flailed in the air. The audience roared with laughter, but Stevie and the goat kept scrambling around in the dirt. She'd finally managed to climb to her feet and grab his stubby little tail when the buzzer sounded. Her time had run out. She let go of the goat and watched as he scampered away to the other side of the ring.

"Nice try, Stevie!" the announcer laughed. "You just gave a whole new meaning to the term *goat wrestling*. Give her a big hand, folks!"

The crowd applauded. "Stevie, are you okay?" Lisa asked worriedly. The goat had mashed Stevie's hat flat, and Stevie wore a thin layer of brown dust from head to toe.

"Yes, I'm fine," she said, rubbing her elbow. "But that sure didn't feel like any normal goat. They must have fed him Mexican jumping beans or something."

"Well, wave to the crowd so they'll know you're all right. Mr. Cate and Polly Shaver and Karen Nicely are all up there cheering for you," Lisa said. "And don't worry about it. The audience loves you, and you've still got three events to go!"

"You're right." Stevie grinned and pushed her hat back into shape. She waved to the crowd, and everyone cheered even more loudly. *Three events to go,* she thought as she walked back to the gates. *And I've got to win at least two of them!*

THE NEXT EVENT was calf roping. Since the grounds crew didn't need to set anything up, Lisa and Carole and Sal stayed on their horses and waited for the action to begin. Carole was to haze the calves just as she had done with the goats, and Lisa was to keep an eye on the riders. Sal clowned and coordinated them from the far end of the ring.

As before, Mary Corona was the first contestant. She bounded out on her pinto mare and roped her calf successfully, but the calf had long, wiggly legs and she lost a lot of time trying to tie them up. The next few contestants did better. Then it was Gabriel's turn. He carefully positioned Napoleon in the gate, then nodded. With the same lightning speed he'd used in the goat wrestling, he roped his calf and had its legs tied almost before Carole and Lisa could blink. They had nothing to do but sit on their horses and watch while he took his hat off and waved again to the cheering crowd.

"Give that young man a hand," the announcer cried as Gabriel and Napoleon made another triumphant circle around the ring. "He's as fast a calf roper as he is a goat wrestler!"

Stevie was next. Carole and Lisa glanced worriedly at each other as she got ready to ride. When she settled down in the gate they turned their attention to the business at hand. With a quick nod, Stevie signaled to open the chute. She and Tumbleweed thundered out of the gate just behind a brown calf that galloped along like a little racehorse. The calf tried to veer off to the right, but Carole rode alongside him and kept him running straight. Stevie began swinging her lasso in a tight circle, and when Tumbleweed had drawn even with the calf's shoulders, she let the noose go. It fell over his head, right on target. Immediately Tumbleweed stopped and began to back up, keeping the rope taut. Stevie leaped off the right side of the saddle and rushed down to the calf. She had no difficulty pulling him over, but his legs flailed as wildly as the goat's, and it took her a long time to tie three of them together. When she finally stood up and held her arms out, her time had almost run out. She looked disappointedly at Lisa and Carole as she got back on Tumbleweed, and when they announced the winners of the event, Gabriel had come in first, Stevie a distant third.

"Uh-oh," Lisa said to Carole after the announcer had read the results. "It's two events to one, in favor of Gabriel. I think Stevie might really be in trouble."

"I know." Carole frowned. "I hate to admit this, but Gabriel is really good. If Stevie doesn't win the pole bending and the quarter-mile race, she's going to be doing something awful."

"Wonder what it will be?" asked Lisa.

"I don't even want to think about it," said Carole with a grimace.

They trotted down to the end of the ring, where Sal was pretending for the crowd that she and Sadie had both fallen asleep. After she ended her bit to a round of applause, she rode over to Carole and Lisa.

"Let's give the horses a rest while they set up for the pole bending," Sal suggested. She removed her oversized polka-dot nightcap and smiled. "Y'all have clowned hard and you've done a terrific job. Why don't you go take a break as well? They won't need us again until after the pole bending. Then we'll do the fake roundup routine, and then it'll be time for the race."

Actually, a rest didn't sound too bad to Carole and Lisa. They had ridden every turn with all the goat-wrestling and calf-roping contestants, plus they had clowned through the barrel race on foot. They dismounted and led Pogo and Ghost over to a water trough, then gave them an armful of hay in a temporary corral. The two girls sat on the fence and ate an apple while the horses munched their hay.

"Look," said Lisa, pointing toward the Rocking S stable. "Here comes Pete."

Carole looked over her shoulder. Pete was crossing the racetrack and heading straight toward them.

"Howdy, girls," he said, tipping his hat. "I saw you two over here and just wondered how everything was going. Are Ghost and Pogo behaving themselves?"

"Oh, yes, Pete, they're terrific," said Carole with a smile. It was true. Whatever the girls had asked them to do, the two quarter horses had done willingly.

Pete watched the grounds crew setting up the poles for the next event. "How's Stevie doing?"

"Well, she won the barrel race," Lisa reported proudly.

"And she came in third in the calf roping," added Carole.

"Then there was the goat wrestling." Lisa shook her head. "Don't ask. You don't even want to know about the goat wrestling."

Pete chuckled. "Those little goats can be right ornery critters." He pushed his hat back on his head. "How's her bet with her boyfriend coming along?"

"Oh, he's not her boyfriend," Lisa explained quickly. "But so far he's ahead two to one. They've got pole bending and the quarter-mile race to go."

78

"Well, if she remembers what I told her about Tumbleweed, she'll do fine," said Pete.

Carole frowned. "What did you tell her?"

"That all she's got to do is touch him with her spurs." Pete chuckled again. "If she does that, he'll outrun every horse in this rodeo."

"I can't imagine that Stevie would forget an important thing like that," Carole said.

"Probably not." He smiled. "Well, you tell her I came by and wished her good luck." He tipped his hat again.

"Thanks, Pete. We will." They watched him as he strolled back to the stable.

"I wonder if Stevie does remember about Tumbleweed and spurs." Carole looked at Lisa. "She's never mentioned it."

"I'm sure she does," Lisa replied. "Stevie's so focused on this rodeo she probably remembers every word that came out of Pete's mouth."

"I guess you're right," agreed Carole. "Let's ride over to the fence. I think the bull riding's about to start."

They remounted Pogo and Ghost and rode over behind the big refreshment trailer to look into the adult arena. The adult rodeo clowns were jumping around in the middle of the ring, loosening up to get ready for the bulls.

"Oh, good!" Carole stood up in her stirrups. "We can watch this until the pole bending begins. It really looks exciting!"

The first cowboy was easing himself down on the back

79

of a brown-and-white bull when Lisa felt someone tapping her leg. She looked down. Eileen was grinning up at her, munching on popcorn.

"You guys are doing a pretty good job of clowning," she said sweetly. "Mr. Cate and Ms. Nicely think you're really funny."

Lisa blinked in surprise. A compliment? From little Eileen? "Thanks, Eileen," she replied. "I'm glad you think so."

"Yeah," Eileen continued. "But the funniest part was when Stevie wrestled that goat and got all dirty. She looked so mad! That's been the best thing about the rodeo so far!"

"Thanks, Eileen," Carole answered sarcastically. "I know Stevie will be glad to hear how much you enjoyed that."

Eileen rattled her popcorn bag. "I know something else that Stevie would enjoy."

"What?" Lisa asked with a frown.

"She would really enjoy knowing my secret." Eileen tossed a piece of popcorn in her mouth and looked up at the girls with an overly sweet smile. "Are you sure you wouldn't like to know, too?"

Lisa and Carole looked at each other and shook their heads. "No thanks, Eileen," Lisa replied. "I don't think we need to know anything you might want to tell us."

"No, really. It's a neat thing." Eileen's green eyes

80

flashed. She chewed her popcorn quickly. "I mean, it's a really *important* thing! It could mean a lot to Stevie."

"Well, if it's that important, why don't you go tell Stevie yourself?" Carole asked.

Eileen pulled on Lisa's big Western stirrup. "Because she was mean to me this morning," she whined, her lower lip stuck out. "She said she was going to rope me and tie me up and make Yankee and Doodle drag me behind the wagon."

"Oh, for Pete's sake, Eileen." Lisa shook her head in disgust. "She was only kidding." She'd started to say something else when a deafening roar went up from the adult side of the arena. A huge buckskin bull with long, pointed horns had just tossed his rider high in the air. The cowboy was scrambling in the dirt, trying to avoid being gored as the bull came charging after him, his horns low and his eyes wild. All the adult clowns were waving their arms and running in circles, desperately trying to distract the angry animal from the fallen cowboy. Every time one of them went near, though, the bull shook his horns and bellowed even more loudly.

"Hold on, boys, I'm coming!" a voice called. Carole and Lisa looked over at their side of the arena. San Antonio Sal had dropped the bouquet of plastic flowers she was clowning with and was running over to help.

"Should we go, too?" Lisa asked as they watched her scramble over the fence.

81

"You two stay right there!" Sal called over to them. "Don't you come near this bull!"

Pulling a huge red scarf from her pocket, she ran full speed toward the snorting bull. The bright, shiny fabric must have caught his eye, because he looked up from the cowboy he was trying to gore and started to run straight at Sal. While another clown helped the shaken cowboy to his feet, Sal flapped her scarf at the bull and lured him toward the barrel, where the barrel man was poking his head up and yelling something at the bull in Spanish. Confused, the angry animal stopped and pawed the ground for a moment, his breath coming in loud snorts. As he tried to decide what to do next, the point clown sneaked along the fence and opened the temporary pen next to the racetrack.

"See if you can get him in here, Sal," the clown called. "I'll head him off this way."

Sal nodded but didn't take her eyes off the bull. "Come on, Bossy," she called to the animal sweetly. "You've already dumped your rider. Now you need to go bye-bye!"

The bull stared at her. She waved her scarf as if she were bidding someone farewell, then twirled it over her head like a lasso. The bull snorted once and ran straight at her, his hooves thundering in the dirt.

"Heads up, everybody!" the barrel man yelled. "Here he comes!"

Still twirling the scarf, Sal ran straight for the open pen. The bull chased her at a hard gallop. As fast as Sal

82

was running, the bull was gaining on her. His horns were not ten feet away from her when she scurried into the pen and scrambled up the fence on the other side. Bellowing loudly, the bull rushed in behind her, and the point clown slammed the pen shut behind him. The stadium erupted in wild cheers.

"Folks, that was San Antonio Sal doing that fancy piece of footwork with that bull," the adult ring announcer said. "Let's give her and all our hardworking rodeo clowns a big hand!"

Sal bounded happily back into the ring and bowed, then ran over and pretended to give the limping cowboy a big kiss. The crowd roared and clapped even harder as she clowned her way back to the junior ring.

"Wow," Carole breathed as Sal climbed back over the fence. "That was really scary!"

"I know," Lisa said shakily. "My heart's beating like crazy. And look. That bull still hasn't calmed down."

Carole looked over at the temporary pen. The bull stood in the middle of it, staring at Sal, still pawing at the ground and bellowing.

"Whew!" Sal said, wiping her forehead as she walked over to the girls. "That was a close one! I didn't think that little ol' temporary fence was going to hold me when I started climbing it! It must be made out of chicken wire!"

"Sal, we were so scared," Lisa said. "I had no idea bulls were that fast."

"They can be when they're mad. Apparently that critter is having a bad rodeo day!" Sal laughed as she caught her breath. "How's the pole bending going?"

Lisa and Carole looked at each other. In all the excitement, they'd totally forgotten about the pole bending contest. Immediately they turned their attention to the junior ring, where Gabriel had just finished.

"Oh, good," Lisa said as the announcer called Stevie's name. "We haven't missed Stevie. I hope she remembers everything Sal taught her about pole bending."

"I do, too," said Carole. "That way she might at least do better at this than she did at goat wrestling. Stevie doesn't need to be the comic relief again!"

The girls watched as Stevie and Tumbleweed positioned themselves behind the starting line. The buzzer sounded, and Tumbleweed leaped forward at a gallop. They twisted around the first pole, then the second. Tumbleweed wove around the poles surefootedly, using all his quarter horse instincts. Carole and Lisa noticed that Stevie leaned back ever so slightly in the saddle when Tumbleweed changed his leads, just the way Sal had told her. They turned around the end pole in a cloud of dust, then began twisting back through the course to the finish line. Stevie's hat flew off her head again as Tumbleweed lengthened his stride into a hard gallop. A cheer went up from the crowd as they finished.

"A mighty fine run for Ms. Stevie Lake!" the announcer called. "Give her a big hand, and we'll have our winners in just a minute."

The crowd clapped for Stevie. Several wild cheers rang out from the wagon train contingent. Lisa and Carole looked at each other, wondering if Stevie had been fast enough to beat Gabriel. If Stevie didn't win this event, there would be no way she could win the rodeo, and her bet with Gabriel would be over.

"Oh, please," Lisa whispered, closing her eyes and crossing her fingers. "Let her win this one!"

Suddenly the ring announcer's voice broke the expectant stillness of the arena. "Ladies and gentlemen," he began. "I'm pleased to announce that this year's pole bending champ is none other than Ms. Stevie Lake from Willow Creek, Virginia!"

Though Carole and Lisa knew they weren't supposed to cheer, they leaned over from their horses and gave each other a hug. Again they could hear Mr. Cate's shrill whistle ringing out over Karen Nicely's wildly clanging cowbell.

"Now they're tied," said Carole. "Whoever wins the quarter-mile race will win it all!"

"GOOD BOY, TUMBLEWEED!" Stevie said to the sweaty quarter horse as she led him to the trough for a long drink of water. From the arena she could hear the rodeo crowd laughing at one of Sal and Lisa and Carole's routines, while just ahead of her a tractor smoothed the surface of the track in preparation for the quarter-mile race. There was a fifteen-minute break, during which the clowns would entertain the crowd and then help them relocate around the track. The break also served as a rest period for the horses and riders who'd competed in the previous events.

"You've been such a good horse!" Stevie reached over and patted Tumbleweed's lathered shoulder as he slurped long swallows of water. "Everything that's gone wrong has been my fault."

86

Stevie knew very well that the day's mistakes had, indeed, been hers. Tumbleweed had performed perfectly, from racing after the goat at just the right speed to holding the calf tightly on the line while Stevie tried to tie his feet. "I guess I'm just not too hot with four-legged nonhorse creatures," she said with a shrug.

She looked at Tumbleweed. "But I'm real good when it's just me alone, and we're great together!" She grinned as Tumbleweed raised his head from the water trough, his chin dripping. "Now we've just got one more event to go. If we can win this race, it won't matter how badly I wrestle goats or rope calves!"

She led Tumbleweed to the concession trailer and leaned against him as Carole and Lisa chased Sal around the arena, trying to rope her with string they squirted out of a can. She smiled as she watched her friends clowning for the crowd and making everyone laugh. "I bet Phil's not doing anything like that right now," she whispered. "I bet he's probably paddling down some river with Meghan or Chelsea or whatever her name is. She's wearing some really cute outfit, and they're probably planning their next vacation together, which will be something really glamorous and exciting, like climbing the Himalayas." Just at that moment Tumbleweed shifted on his feet and gave a big sigh. "I know exactly how you feel, boy," Stevie said sadly as she rubbed the horse behind his ears.

"Hi, Stevie."

Stevie looked up to see Eileen, dressed in her pioneer clothes and holding a cone of pink cotton candy.

"Hi, Eileen," she replied.

"I saw you try to wrestle that little goat. You were pretty funny. Everybody laughed at you."

"Oh, really?" Stevie's cheeks started to burn—not at the thought of the crowd laughing at her, but at the thought of Mr. Hotshot Rodeo Star Gabriel laughing at her.

"Yes, it was *really* funny." Eileen bit into her cotton candy. "I laughed the hardest."

"I bet you did, Eileen." Stevie took off her cowboy hat and wiped the sweat from her forehead.

"You know, I still know that secret," Eileen began again.

"What secret?"

"The one I tried to tell you this morning."

Stevie frowned. "You mean when you came over to the wagon and bugged us while we were trying to get ready?"

Eileen nodded.

"I thought you were making up that secret business just to be a pest."

"No," said Eileen. "I really do have a secret."

"Sorry, Eileen." Stevie turned back toward Tumbleweed. "I don't think you could possibly know anything that I would be the least bit interested in learning."

"You never know," Eileen taunted her. "I mean, I

might know something that you might need to know, because if you didn't, something terrible might happen."

"Go watch the rodeo, Eileen," Stevie said as she checked Tumbleweed's right front shoe. "Go see what the clowns are doing."

"And then if something terrible happened and you didn't know because you hadn't bothered to ask . . ."

"Eileen, I—"

"And then you'd really feel horrible if—"

"All right!" Stevie said so sharply that Tumbleweed jumped. "I give up! Eileen, whatever this vitally important secret is, please, just go ahead and spit it out now!"

Eileen started to poke out her lower lip in her usual pout but then changed her mind. "Okay." She took a step toward Stevie and spoke just above a whisper. "This is what I overheard Gabriel telling Shelly Bean at lunch the other day. He told Shelly that you two had a bet, and whoever won the most rodeo events would get to make the other perform a secret dare."

Stevie rolled her eyes and slapped her hat back on her head. "Sorry, Eileen, but that's old news. I was there when we made the bet. I already know all that stuff."

"But wait. There's more. I heard what Gabriel's secret dare is!" Eileen's green eyes glittered.

Stevie looked at Eileen and frowned. As much as she disliked the idea of getting any information at all from this bratty little girl, Gabriel's secret dare was something worth knowing. "What?" she finally asked reluctantly.

Eileen grinned. "Gabriel's going to dare you to be his date for the big barbecue dinner tonight, and he wants to make you rush up and give him a big kiss when he accepts his first-prize award!"

"What?" Stevie was stunned. She grew first hot, then cold, and her head spun. This was far worse than anything she had ever imagined! She had thought she would just make Gabriel put on her pioneer dress and milk Veronica. She figured he would make her do something like saying over and over that he was the best rodeo rider in the world while she cleaned out Napoleon's stall. She had no idea Gabriel would want to make her kiss him! And worse, in front of everybody!

No way! She turned and furiously checked all the buckles on Tumbleweed's tack. Nohow! She smoothed Tumbleweed's saddle blanket and gave him a brisk pat on his rump. They were going to win this race. Even if she had to carry Tumbleweed across the finish line on her back, she would do it to avoid having to kiss Gabriel!

"All quarter-mile racers, please report to the track," said the ring announcer's voice.

Stevie hopped up on Tumbleweed. She looked down at Eileen, whose mouth was now ringed with pink cotton-candy stains. "Thanks, Eileen. You've just let me know how much is at stake in this race."

"So it was a pretty good secret, huh?" Eileen asked proudly.

"Eileen, it was one of the best I've heard in a long time. Now go find your parents and watch me beat Gabriel."

"Oh, goody!" Eileen said as she scurried off to the grandstand.

Stevie and Tumbleweed trotted over to the starting line, steering clear of the angry bull, which was still snorting at everyone who came near his pen. Stevie saw that Carole and Lisa and Sal were clowning on horseback, leading the crowd from the arena stands and out toward the track so that they could watch the race more closely. Lisa and Sal had exited the grandstand at the far end of the arena while Carole had ridden out closer to Stevie. She and Pogo stood between the starting line and the pen that held the cantankerous bull. Stevie waved at Carole, who waved back and then started making kicking motions with her feet. Stevie frowned and looked down at her boots. What was Carole trying to tell her? Had she stepped on a candy wrapper or something?

"Riders, take your places behind the starting line, please!" A man wearing a black ten-gallon hat was speaking through a bullhorn. Stevie forgot about her boots and trotted Tumbleweed up to a tape that stretched across the track. Mary Corona, riding her pinto, was already there, as were some riders Stevie didn't recognize. She was just beginning to wonder where Gabriel was when she heard a familiar voice behind her.

"Hey, Miss I Can Pin a Goat to the Ground in Eight

Seconds! How's it going?" Gabriel laughed and pulled Napoleon up right beside her. Stevie had never realized how much bigger Napoleon was than Tumbleweed, and how his coat seemed to glitter like gold in the sun. Gabriel reined him back a little. "I had no idea you were going to go for laughs in the goat wrestling. I thought your friends were supposed to be the clowns today!"

"They needed some help in that event, Mr. Can't Bend a Pole or Race a Barrel Too Fast," Stevie snapped back. "The crowd was getting bored with a certain contestant taking all these grand tours of the arena, waving to them on his golden palomino!"

"They seemed to like it," Gabriel replied. "Although I have to admit, it wasn't as funny as watching you and that goat flop around in the dust!" He laughed again and eyed Stevie's filthy cowboy shirt. "Too bad about your nice clean shirt."

"Too bad about yours, too," she said sadly.

"Mine?" Gabriel frowned and looked down at his almost spotless white shirt.

"Yeah." Stevie grinned. "In about two minutes it's going to be covered in my dust when this race begins. By the time we cross the finish line, you'll be able to write your initials across it!"

"Oh, right," Gabriel snorted. "In your dreams." He pulled his hat down over his eyes and gave Napoleon's golden shoulder a pat.

"More like in my nightmares if you've got anything to

92

do with them," Stevie snapped back, getting mad all over again at the idea of him making her kiss him.

"Riders, get ready to go!" the man with the bullhorn announced. "Halfway around the track is a quarter mile." He lifted the starting gun.

Suddenly the riders grew silent and concentrated on the stretch of track ahead of them. Even the horses quivered with anticipation, eager to burst down the track as fast as they could go. Farther away, by the first turn, Stevie could see Sal and Lisa sitting on their horses, looking toward them, waiting for the race to begin. How proud they would be when she won! She leaned low and forward in the saddle and grasped the reins tightly, waiting for the blast of the starting gun. She had turned her head one last time to shoot a menacing scowl at Gabriel when suddenly an odd movement caught her eye. Just behind Carole and Pogo, the angry bull was hooking the flimsy fence with his horns. The fence wobbled, then sagged to the ground. The bull was free! He leaped forward and pawed the ground once as he sniffed the air, then lowered his head and began to charge. And he began to charge straight at Carole and Pogo!

THE CRACK OF the starting gun split the air. All the other horses sprang forward. Tumbleweed's first impulse was to do the same, but Stevie reined him hard to the left. Immediately he obeyed, pivoting with his quarter horse agility.

"Come on, Tumbleweed!" She squeezed with her legs and urged him forward, faster than she'd ever wanted him to go before, but he seemed stuck in his regular lope. Though it was fast, it wasn't nearly fast enough to get to Carole in time.

"Come on, Tumbleweed," she said again. She leaned closer to him and squeezed him again, but it did no good. It was as if he were stuck going fifty miles an hour when he could easily have gone eighty. Then Stevie remembered something Pete had told her. "Don't use your spurs on

94

Tumbleweed unless you want him to take off like a rocket."
Your spurs! That was what Carole had been trying to signal
her right before the race! Instantly Stevie jammed her
heels into Tumbleweed's side. He hesitated for an instant,
then leaped across the track faster than he'd ever gone
before. His flying mane whipped Stevie's face, but she
maintained her race position—low and forward in the saddle. Some of the spectators, astonished by her actions, were
just beginning to realize what was happening. Several people had seen the bull and began running away from the
track, their children clutched in their arms.

From the corner of her eye, Stevie could see that Lisa
and Sal had also spotted the trouble Carole was in and
had begun to race toward her. The other rodeo clowns
were scrambling from the adult arena to help, and the
pickup cowboys were galloping to the exit at the end of
the arena. Still, Stevie was closest to the bull. She was the
only one who could reach Carole in time.

Tumbleweed was now halfway across the track. Though
Carole and Pogo were trying to side-pass around the bull,
he had them trapped in the corner between the grandstand and the back of the concession trailer. They had no
room to maneuver, and his deadly horns were getting
closer and closer. Carole kept Pogo moving from side to
side, but Stevie could already see the whites showing
around Pogo's terrified eyes. If Pogo grew any more fright-
ened, she could panic and buck Carole off, leaving her
totally defenseless in front of the bull.

Frantically, Stevie racked her brain. Why hadn't she listened when Carole and Lisa had talked about clowning? What had they said clowns did when bulls went crazy? Banged on a barrel or something like that. But Stevie had no barrel to bang on. All she had was Tumbleweed and herself. "Think!" she whispered as they thundered closer to the bull. "Think!"

Stevie was almost there. She could see white foam curling from Pogo's mouth. She jammed her heels into Tumbleweed's side again. He bore down and went even faster. "Hey!" Stevie screamed at the bull at the top of her lungs. "Hey! Bossy! Over here!"

The bull paid no attention. He kept moving closer and closer to Carole, now snorting, now shaking his horns from side to side. "Hey!" Stevie yelled again. Then she spied Sal's big red scarf lying on the ground. Sal must have dropped it after she'd lured the bull into the pen the first time around. If that scarf had worked with this bull once, maybe it would work again.

Stevie shifted her weight slightly to the left and leaned low in the saddle, using the same motions she'd used when she was trying to slide off Tumbleweed on top of the goat. Instinctively Tumbleweed veered slightly to the left, carrying Stevie closer to the scarf. In all her life she'd never leaned so low to the ground on horseback before, but with one swooping motion, clinging to the saddle horn, she stretched her left arm out as far as it would go. Her fingertips grazed the silky red material. She stretched to her absolute limit and tried to grab it. She got it! She clutched it in her hand as she pulled herself back into the saddle and urged Tumbleweed forward again. She wondered for a moment whether Tumbleweed would sense Pogo's fear and balk at running so close to the bull. Most horses would flee from an animal that was snorting and bellowing in rage. But the little quarter horse didn't flinch. He galloped on, obeying her commands without question.

Stevie pointed him straight at the bull's side, then reined him up about ten feet away. "Hey, Ferdinand!" Stevie yelled at the bull. "Look at this!" She flapped the red scarf. The bull saw it out of the corner of his eye and turned to look. For a moment his vicious horns pointed away from Carole and Pogo.

"Hey, Ferdinand!" Stevie called again. *"Toro, toro, toro!"* She loosened her grip on Tumbleweed's reins and held the scarf out beside her the way a bullfighter would hold a cape. Jiggling one end of the scarf, she waved it back and forth in front of the bull. He looked at it for a moment, then turned the rest of his huge body to face it. That gave Carole and Pogo enough room to leap out of the corner where they'd been trapped. Carole stopped Pogo just beyond the reach of the bull's horns, then began to wave her derby at him from the other direction.

For a few more seconds the girls worked hard to keep the bull flustered. The bull didn't know which one to try to gore first, so he just stood there, shaking his horns at both of them and pawing the ground. After what seemed like hours, the adult team of rodeo clowns made it through the grandstand. They jumped around and further confused the bull, then joined hands and made a shield in front of Stevie and Carole while the two cowboys arrived and threw lassos around the bull's neck. Finally realizing he was outnumbered and roped, the bull gave one last bellow and allowed the cowboys to lead him back to the main stock trailer.

"Are you girls okay?" one of the clowns asked after the bull had been led away.

"I think so." Stevie looked at Carole and Pogo. They both seemed shaken.

"Maybe you two should go and take it easy for a little while," the clown suggested. "Petunia can be a handful when he gets riled up, but you two did a great job containing him."

Stevie frowned. "That bull's name is Petunia?"

The clown shrugged. "So go figure. I guess whoever named him didn't know too much about cattle."

"Whatever." Stevie chuckled with relief. She handed Sal's red scarf to the clown and trotted over to Carole. "Are you okay?"

"I think so," said Carole. "But let's go somewhere else. Pogo and I need to get as far away from Petunia as we possibly can."

The two girls rode over to Lisa and Sal. Though it

seemed to Stevie that the whole incident had taken hours, in reality it had ended in less than a minute. Lisa and Sal had galloped at full speed from the other end of the track, and they were just now arriving.

"Stevie! Carole! Are you two all right?" Lisa looked sickly pale. Her eyes were wide with fear.

"We're okay," said Stevie, although her mouth was dry and her heart was thumping like a drum.

"You two sure did a great job of bull wrangling!" Sal said, beaming at them.

"Thanks," Carole said. "Now I think I'd like to sit down a minute."

Everyone dismounted, giving the horses a well-deserved rest. Carole soothed the still-trembling Pogo while Stevie rubbed Tumbleweed affectionately behind his ears. He had done a wonderfully brave job.

"I was so scared," Lisa said, her voice shaking. "Sal and I came as soon as we saw what was happening." She looked at Carole and Stevie with tears in her eyes. "That bull had you trapped! Both of you and the horses could have been killed!"

"I suppose." Stevie took her cowboy hat off. "It's funny, but that didn't occur to me until the clowns led that bull away."

"Me neither," added Carole. She grinned at Stevie. "I kept wondering what you were going to do if he decided to charge that scarf!"

Stevie laughed. "I hadn't figured that out yet." She

looked at Carole quizzically. "Hey, were you trying to tell me to use my heels on Tumbleweed right before the race?"

Carole nodded. "Pete came by to wish you luck and hoped you'd remember what he'd told you about Tumbleweed and spurs."

"I couldn't figure out what you meant until we were halfway across the track," Stevie said. "But I'm glad I remembered it when I did!"

"I'm glad you did, too!" Lisa shook her head. "You two nearly gave me a heart attack!"

"Then let's have a group hug and be grateful we've got lucky stars," suggested Stevie, holding her arms open wide.

The three girls clutched each other, happy that they were all alive and unhurt. Sal joined in, grabbing a handful of tiny silver stars from one of her deep clown pockets and sprinkling them over the girls. They had just begun to laugh about how funny Stevie looked with stars in her damp, tousled hair when Gabriel rode up on Napoleon.

"Hi," he said, reining the big palomino in close. He hopped off and pulled the reins over Napoleon's head. "I just heard what happened with the bull. Are you okay, Carole?"

"Yes, I am, thanks to Stevie." Carole smiled.

"And are you okay?" Gabriel turned to Stevie and for once looked at her without a teasing expression.

"I'm fine, thanks," she replied. Suddenly she remembered that this whole thing had started right as she was beginning the quarter-mile race—the event that would decide who won their bet. "Hey," she said. "Who won the race? I kind of got distracted and forgot all about it."

"Oh, haven't you heard?" Gabriel asked, his old teasing grin returning. "Me, of course. I beat Mary Corona by half a length." He stuck his thumbs in the belt loops of his jeans. "Which means that I won three out of the five events. Which means that I also won the rodeo and our bet!"

Stevie stood still. Her face grew hot with embarrassment at having been beaten, but then she smiled. She had lost the rodeo fair and square, but she had lost it for a good reason—helping to save her friend. There was nothing to be ashamed of about that.

"You're absolutely right," she told Gabriel graciously. "Congratulations!"

She held out her hand. Gabriel took it and they shook.

"Now," Stevie said. "What is it that you want me to do?"

"Oh, how about I tell you later?" he replied with another impish grin, his blue eyes looking bluer than ever.

"Okay." Stevie gulped, her palms growing sweaty. "When?"

"How about tonight? Just before the big barbecue dinner?"

"That's fine." Stevie tried to smile through the butterflies that were beginning to flit in her stomach. "I can hardly wait to hear what you've dreamed up."

"STEVIE, WHAT A wonderful rescue you accomplished today!" Mr. Cate stopped behind Stevie's chair, put one arm around her shoulders, and gave her a squeeze. He looked over at Gabriel, who was sitting beside her, beaming proudly. "You did a great rodeo job, too, young man," Mr. Cate added with a grin. Then he noticed the two empty plates on the table in front of them.

"You guys know you can get seconds on the barbecue, don't you?" Mr. Cate clutched his own second helping in his free hand, balancing a large plate piled high with barbecued ribs, corn bread, and a thick slice of apple pie.

Stevie smiled at her old friend from the wagon train. "Thanks, Mr. Cate. I think I may go get some more pie. It's really delicious!"

"Would you like me to go with you?" Gabriel asked, rising from his chair. "Or I could bring you a piece."

"No, thanks," said Stevie. "I can do it by myself."

She walked to the back of the room, where a large buffet table was covered with huge platters of food. In one corner of the room, a band consisting of a guitarist, a fiddler, and an accordionist played over the happy hum of wagon train pioneers and rodeo riders laughing and talking. Stevie put a hefty slice of apple pie on her plate and walked back to her seat next to Gabriel. She shot Carole and Lisa a dirty look when they giggled as Gabriel rose and pulled Stevie's chair out for her. The next thing she knew, a camera flash popped. Polly Shaver had snapped their picture together. Stevie smiled broadly, then started in on her pie.

Gabriel watched as she ate. "You know, I really didn't mean to make fun of you quite so hard over the goat wrestling contest," he said suddenly, his voice cracking.

"That's okay." Stevie shrugged. "I guess it was pretty funny."

"And I didn't really mean it when I said the only rodeo event you'd be good at was the cow chip tossing contest," he continued.

"Don't worry about it," Stevie said through a mouthful of pie.

"And when I said that—"

"Look." Stevie swallowed and looked at him. "We both

said some really stupid things. We both got on each other's nerves. But it's okay. When you offered to call the rodeo a draw and not hold me to our bet, that made up for everything."

"Well, it seemed like the least I could do after you saved Carole from that bull," he mumbled, suddenly staring hard at his glass of iced tea.

"It's just too bad we'll never find out how bad Tumbleweed could have beaten Napoleon," Stevie said.

Gabriel turned quickly in his chair to say something back. Then he saw that she was smiling. "Okay," he laughed. "You got me on that one."

Stevie returned her attention to her pie. In a way it was a shame that she and Tumbleweed had not competed in the race. Tumbleweed was incredibly fast once you put your spurs to him, and it would have been fun to find out which horse could have won. Still, she had no regrets about what she'd done. If anything had happened to Carole or Pogo because she wanted to compete in a horse race . . . well, she didn't even want to think about that. And it had been nice of Gabriel to walk over to their wagon and offer to call it a draw. Stevie stole a glance at him out of the corner of her eye. *Thank goodness I won't have to kiss him in front of all these people*, she thought, her palms growing sweaty all over again.

"Hey, check out those two!" Carole whispered to Lisa. They were sitting a few seats down the table from Stevie and Gabriel.

104

"I know." Lisa glanced over at them. "For once they actually seem to be enjoying each other's company instead of boasting about who's better or faster or stronger."

Carole giggled. "Look at the way Stevie's smiling at him!"

"And look at the way he's smiling back!" Lisa winked. "I think they both have huge, world-class crushes on each other."

"I think you're right."

"And why not?" continued Lisa. "They're both neat people. We already know what a wonderful person Stevie is. And even though Gabriel can be an arrogant know-it-all, he's got some good points, too."

Carole nodded. "He's got those killer blue eyes, he knows everything about the Oregon Trail, he rides like a dream, plus he's helping us with our notes for Deborah's newspaper assignment."

Lisa smiled. "With all the information he's given us, we should have an awesome outline for Deborah by the time we get back to Willow Creek."

Just then Mr. Williams, the president of the rodeo association, stood up at the head table. "Ladies and gentlemen," he said into a large microphone. "It's now time to present the rodeo awards. Please come forward when your name is called and collect your prize."

The crowd cheered. Several cowboys gave earsplitting whistles that echoed around the room. All eyes were on Mr. Williams at the podium.

The adult prizes were given out first. One cowboy who was dressed all in black took the award for the bronc riding contest. Another came up in a fringed buckskin jacket to accept the bull riding prize. Several other awards were passed out, and then the cowboy who'd won the most points overall was called onstage. Mr. Williams shook his hand, presented him with a check for $500, and then handed him a huge gold belt buckle that had a bucking horse stamped on it. The crowd cheered while the cowboy looked at the audience with tears in his eyes.

"I know five hundred dollars is a lot of money," he said. "But I'll spend that pretty fast. This belt buckle I'll treasure the rest of my life! Thanks a lot!"

Everyone clapped as he sat down. Mr. Williams took the microphone again.

"Next we have our junior riders. This year's competition was fierce, but our overall junior rodeo champ is Gabriel Jackson from the Wagons West trail ride." Mr. Williams looked out into the audience. "Come on up here, Gabriel, and get your prize."

Polly's camera flashed again as Gabriel rose from his chair and walked to the podium. Mr. Williams shook his hand, then gave him a long blue ribbon and a gold trophy with a bronc rider on top. Gabriel grinned and looked very proud.

"Give that young cowboy a big hand, folks!" Mr. Williams said as Gabriel made his way back to the table.

106

Stevie looked wistfully at the shining bronc rider on the top of his trophy as he sat beside her. It would have been neat, she thought, if she could have brought a trophy home to show Max and Deborah and her family.

"Now, we have something special for you folks tonight," Mr. Williams continued. "Normally we don't do anything like this, but normally we don't have anything like this happen. There is someone very special sitting in our audience tonight who this afternoon exhibited an extraordinary amount of courage and bravery. Would Ms. Stevie Lake please come forward?"

Stevie looked questioningly at Carole and Lisa as everyone turned to smile at her. She frowned. What was all this about?

"Go, Stevie," Polly whispered from across the table. "They're waiting for you! I'll take your picture!"

Stevie rose from her chair and walked to the podium.

"Ladies and gentlemen, for the one or two of you who might not have heard, we had a dangerous and regrettable incident with one of our bulls this afternoon when he escaped a stock pen and cornered one of our clowns. Even though Stevie was already lined up for the quarter-mile race, she saw what was happening and rushed over to save her friend, Carole Hanson." Mr. Williams put his arm around Stevie's shoulders. "Stevie, we thank you for your quick thinking and your courage, and we'd like to present you with this in honor of your bravery."

Mr. Williams held out a small black box. Stevie opened

it. Inside was a golden belt buckle just like the one the champion cowboy had won. "Gosh," she breathed, awed by the beautiful gift. "Thanks."

"Hold it up so that everyone can see, Stevie," Mr. Williams suggested.

Stevie grinned and held the belt buckle high above her head. The whole audience stood up and cheered. Stevie could see Carole and Lisa and Mr. Cate and Polly all clapping for her. Jeremy Barksdale and Karen Nicely and even little Eileen cheered as well. Then she saw a figure climb up on a chair. It was Gabriel, clapping hardest of all.

"Hey, Stevie," he yelled above the applause. "Catch this!" He stopped clapping and with one hand blew her a big kiss. Everyone in the audience roared!

Stevie's face reddened with embarrassment. How could Gabriel do that! Everyone knew they'd practically been at each other's throats throughout the expedition, and now he was blowing her kisses. She turned away from the cheering crowd and shook Mr. Williams's hand. By the time she returned to her seat, Gabriel had gone to help the men clear away some of the tables for square dancing.

"Hey, Stevie, let's see what they gave you!" Carole and Lisa grabbed the chairs on either side of Stevie. She laid the belt buckle on the white tablecloth, where it glowed gold in the soft light. Stevie turned it over. Mr. Williams had explained that her name and the date would be engraved on the back.

"Wow," said Lisa. "It's just like that cowboy said. You can keep this forever."

"You sure can." Carole ran a finger over the buckle. "You can always remember that this was the day you saved my life!"

"Oh, I'll remember a lot about this day," said Stevie. "I'll remember you guys and Tumbleweed and San Antonio Sal . . ."

"And Gabriel," teased Lisa.

"Yes, and Gabriel," Stevie admitted with a smile. "You know, I think you guys were right. He and I do have a mutual crush going. As much as I hated the idea of having to kiss him in front of everybody, I'll have to admit that I do kind of wonder what it might have been like."

"So, what's stopping you?" laughed Carole. "The party's just beginning."

Stevie rubbed the belt buckle. "I don't know. I guess I'm not really, *really* interested in him." She shrugged. "I mean, he's cute and good-looking and he has a lot of nice qualities, but he can't hold a candle to Phil."

"But, Stevie, you've worried that your relationship with Phil was over ever since we started this trip," said Lisa. "You've convinced yourself that he's fallen for another girl."

"I know." Stevie sighed. "I just realized when I saw Gabriel blow me that kiss that he and I have really been flirting with each other the whole time. Oh, I know that competing in contests and calling each other names

109

doesn't seem like flirting, but in this case, that's what it was." She looked at her friends. "And if I can flirt with Gabriel, how can I expect Phil not to flirt with that cute redhead who's on the raft with him? I mean, it wouldn't be fair!"

Carole and Lisa looked at each other and shook their heads. Only Stevie Lake could stew for a whole week about Phil Marsten, grumble about Gabriel Jackson, get herself bamboozled by a goat, save Carole's life, and then decide that she'd had a crush on Gabriel all along and she didn't mind if Phil flirted with a cute redhead who probably didn't even exist!

Carole gave a low whistle. "Stevie," she said, "when you want to, you sure can cover a lot of ground!"

Just then the band played a single loud chord and Mr. Williams turned the microphone back on. "Okay, everybody. Now Dashing Dan and His Prairie Dog Band are going to provide music for square dancing. All the tables up front have been cleared away, so grab a partner and form your squares!"

Jeremy Barksdale came over and asked Lisa to dance, while a cute boy who'd competed in the calf roping contest grabbed Carole's hand. As Stevie watched her friends join the dancers, she felt a tap on her shoulder.

"May I have this dance, ma'am?"

Stevie turned. Gabriel, smiling, was holding his arm out for her. She rose and took it, and together they walked to the dance floor.

"I've got to admit this is the first time I've ever danced with a girl who had a championship rodeo belt buckle," Gabriel said as they joined hands for a large Texas star.

"Well, this is the first time I've ever danced with a boy who could pin a goat in eight seconds," Stevie laughed.

"And tie a calf in ten," he added. "And win the quarter-mile race in—"

"Okay, okay," said Stevie. "It's just a shame that we'll never know who would have really won the rodeo."

Gabriel smiled. "Oh, I don't know," he said as he put his arm snugly around her waist and swung her in a tight circle. "I kind of think we both did."

12

"ISN'T IT WONDERFUL to be home?" Lisa sat on a bale of hay outside Pine Hollow Stables. It was late afternoon, and the girls were watching their horses graze in the front paddock. "I mean, we've got hot showers and soft beds and regular clothes and milk that comes out of a refrigerator instead of out of a cow!"

Carole looked up from the stack of photographs in her lap and laughed. "Gosh, Lisa. I thought you were really getting into the pioneer spirit."

"Oh, don't get me wrong. I mean, I really enjoyed the trip and the rodeo and all the people we met," Lisa said. "I guess I just learned a lot about myself, too."

"Like what?" asked Carole.

"Like even though it's neat to do things the way the

112

pioneers did them, I really like living today a whole lot better."

"I know what you mean," said Carole. "Experiencing the past is great, but it's the modern age we've got to deal with today."

"I wonder if she has brown eyes or green eyes?" Stevie worried out loud as she tapped her foot nervously in the dust.

Carole frowned. "Who?"

"Phil's new girlfriend," Stevie said morosely, cupping her chin in her hand.

"Maybe she's got one of each," suggested Lisa. "There's a girl in my class like that. It's really cool."

"Or maybe she's got one of all three," Carole laughed. "One blue, one green, and one brown, right in the middle of her forehead! That would certainly get Phil's attention."

"Ha, ha, ha," Stevie said while her friends collapsed in giggles beside her. "You two don't seem to be taking this nearly as seriously as I am."

"I'm sorry, Stevie." Lisa wiped tears of laughter from her eyes. "It's just that this wonderful, beautiful, incredibly smart girl is all you've thought about ever since we've been back. Haven't you talked to Phil about her on the phone?"

"No. We've just played phone tag with each other. I leave him a message, and then he leaves me one back."

Stevie checked her watch. "He's supposed to be here in five minutes to go with us to TD's."

"Good," said Carole. "In five minutes we'll probably find out that this mysterious redhead is just a product of your overactive imagination, and we can talk about something else for a change."

"Like what?" asked Stevie.

"Like how much Deborah liked the outline we did for her," said Lisa. "You know, she seemed really surprised. I don't think she thought we would come up with something that good."

"Well, we had a lot of help with it," Carole said. "We had the photos Polly Shaver gave us, and Gabriel helped, too. He told us a bunch of historical stuff that was really neat." Carole held up one of the snapshots. "Look, Lisa. Here's that picture Polly took of you milking Veronica!"

The girls looked at the picture. Veronica the cow stood gazing at the camera while Lisa grinned from the milking stool.

"I'm going to hang that up over Veronica diAngelo's cubby," Lisa laughed as she studied the picture more closely. "I think she needs to know that somewhere out West, walking the Oregon Trail, is a perfectly nice cow that shares her name."

"I wonder what her name is?" Stevie said glumly.

Carole frowned and waved the picture. "Stevie, it's Veronica! Don't you remember?"

"No, not the cow. Phil's new girlfriend. I used to think

it was probably Meghan or Chelsea, but now I'm leaning toward Kelli. Or maybe Jennifer."

"*Arrrggghhhh!*" groaned Carole. "I give up!"

"Look!" Stevie cried. "Here he comes!"

The girls watched as the Marstens' station wagon slowly rolled up the Pine Hollow driveway. Lisa and Carole exchanged smiles.

"I think now would be the perfect time to pin this picture over Veronica's cubby," Carole suggested with a wink.

"I think you're absolutely right." Lisa nodded vigorously. "This scene might be too awful for our tender eyes to see." Quietly they tiptoed back inside the stable.

"Phil!" Stevie cried, running toward him as soon as he was out of the car.

"Hi, Stevie!" he called, hurrying to meet her.

They met halfway between the stable and the driveway and gave each other a big hug.

"It's so good to see you!" said Phil, grinning down at her. His trip had left him with a much deeper tan and a peeling nose, but otherwise he looked the same. His eyes still twinkled and his smile was still warm.

"Oh, me too," Stevie replied with a grin. "Did you have a good vacation?"

"It was terrific," he said. "How about yours?"

"Oh, it was so much fun! We got out there and we were assigned roles to play and we had to wear period costumes, which meant I had to drive a team of horses all day in a dress! Lisa was in charge of this cow named Veronica, and Carole stayed in the saddle from sunup till dusk." The words seemed to tumble out of Stevie's mouth.

"Then there was this bratty little kid named Eileen, and her teddy bear was the only thing we couldn't pull out of the river when her wagon got swamped. Then she cried over it so hard that she started a cattle stampede, and we had to jump on these cowponies bareback and—"

Phil's green eyes grew wide. He laughed. "Stevie! Slow down! You're making your vacation sound like a Wild West movie!"

"Well, it was, in a way." Stevie stopped and took a breath. "We met some really neat people on the trip, too. There was Jeremy Barksdale, the wagon master; Mr. Cate from Alabama; Polly Shaver from Cincinnati; Gabri—" Stevie stopped abruptly. In the excitement of seeing Phil, she'd forgotten all about Gabriel. But suddenly his blue eyes and his dimples popped into her head, right along with the beautiful redhead with whom she'd pictured Phil rafting down the river. *Now is the time*, she thought, summoning her courage as they strolled hand in hand to the stable. *I'm going to find out about Phil's new love.*

"But that's enough about my trip," she said, squeezing his hand and gazing up at him adoringly. "Tell me about yours."

"Well, we met up with our outfitters at Rattlesnake

116

Junction. We had a flotilla of four rafts, each carrying twelve people. Every raft had a guide in it, because some of the white water was pretty rough. Our raft capsized twice, and my mom lost her favorite pair of sunglasses." Phil shuddered. "And man, when you got washed overboard you really felt it. That water was cold!"

"Who went with you?" Stevie asked innocently.

"Our guide was Hank Parker. He's been rafting for years, and he knew all the best places along the river to stop. He had this really neat fishing rod that folded up small enough to carry in your shirt pocket."

"Really?" Stevie pretended to be impressed with the fishing rod. "Who else went along?"

"Huh?" Phil looked at her and frowned. "Well, let's see. There were some newlyweds from Atlanta and some retired people from Arizona, and there was the Lin family. They'd flown all the way over from Taiwan just to go rafting."

"That's great, but was there anybody really interesting on your raft?" Stevie persisted.

"Sure. We rode with Mr. Feeney, who recited poetry every time we paddled through rapids; and a guy named Chip, who I played Hacky Sack with, and . . ." Phil thought a minute, then broke into a wide grin. "And there was Red."

"Red?" Stevie repeated weakly.

"Yes. Red." Phil's eyes took on a dreamy look. "Man, she is great."

117

"Great?" Stevie's stomach grew queasy. She had been right all along!

"Yeah. She is so cool. And so smart. We played ball for hours. She even likes soccer and she can swim like a fish." Phil gave a little laugh. "And she loves barbecued potato chips!"

"Potato chips?" Stevie frowned, her face now growing red with anger.

"Yeah, she's great. Every night after supper we would fool around for hours. Then, when we were both exhausted, she'd jump into my arms and give me a big kiss!"

Stevie suddenly dropped Phil's hand. She turned to him, her eyes blazing. "You've got a lot of nerve, Phil Marsten! First you come over here pretending to have missed me, then you start telling me about this wonderful redhead who leaps into your arms and kisses you every night!"

Stevie turned on her heel and walked toward the paddock, where Belle was happily browsing through the grass. Horses, she thought, were dependable. Guys were not.

She heard footsteps following her. "Wait, Stevie," she heard Phil call. "It's not what you think!"

He hurried up behind her and tapped her on the shoulder. "Hey," he said with a laugh. "Red's nobody to be upset about. Red's a dog!"

Stevie whirled around to face him. "Phil Marsten, that's an even jerkier thing to say! Now you're going to tell me that even though this girl is wonderful and funny

118

and smart, you really couldn't like her because she's not very pretty! I think you're the shallowest person I've ever met!"

"No, wait, Stevie," Phil protested. He dropped to the ground, held his hands up like paws, and pretended to pant. "Red really *is* a dog!" he cried. "Like *arf, arf!* Like fetch! Like roll over and play dead!"

Stevie looked down at Phil. Though she was still mad at him, it was hard not to laugh at his goofy dog imitation. "Really?" she said, raising one eyebrow.

He leaped to his feet. "Yes. She's Mr. Feeney's Irish setter. I can show you pictures of her. You can ask my mom and dad."

"Really?" Stevie repeated.

He nodded.

"Oh, Phil," she said. She threw her arms around his neck.

"You know, I'm surprised you'd think I would go rafting and fall for somebody else." Phil sounded hurt.

"I'm sorry," she said as she hugged him. "The whole time I was gone it just seemed so real. And the more I thought about it, the more real it became." She looked at him. "And you *were* involved with a redhead, in a way."

"I know." Phil sighed. "It'll be tough waking up every morning without those big brown eyes looking into mine, begging me to throw a stick!"

"Oh, I think you'll get over it," Stevie laughed, hugging him harder. They stayed like that for a long time.

119

A little farther away, Lisa and Carole tiptoed to the front of the stable.

"How's it going?" Lisa asked, not daring to look at Stevie and Phil.

Carole peeked around the stable door. "It's okay," she reported after a long moment. "They're hugging. They're kissing. If the redhead ever existed, they seem to have gotten over her." She turned to Lisa and grinned. "I think it's safe to come out now!"

"Good!" Lisa sighed with relief. "Now we can go to TD's. Now Stevie will stop talking about the redhead. Now life as we know it will return to normal."

"Terrific." Carole laughed. "It really is wonderful to be home!"

ABOUT THE AUTHOR

BONNIE BRYANT is the author of over a hundred books for young readers, including novelisations of movie hits such as *Teenage Mutant Ninja Turtles*™ and *Honey, I Blew Up the Kids*, written under her married name, B. B. Hiller.

Ms Bryant began writing The Saddle Club in 1986. Although she had done some riding before that, she intensified her studies then and found herself learning right along with her characters Stevie, Carole, and Lisa. She claims that they are all much better riders than she is.

Ms Bryant was born and raised in New York City. She lives in Greenwich Village with her two sons.

the Saddle Club

Collect the series

Value editions — two books in one...

1 Horse Crazy + Horse Shy
2 Horse Sense + Horse Power
3 Trail Mates + Dude Ranch
4 Horse Play + Horse Show
5 Hoof Beat + Riding Camp
6 Horse Wise + Rodeo Rider
7 Starlight Christmas + Sea Horse
8 Team Play + Horse Games
9 Horsenapped + Pack Trip
10 Star Rider + Snow Rider
11 Racehorse + Fox Hunt
12 Horse Trouble + Ghost Rider
13 Show Horse + Beach Ride
14 Bridle Path + Stable Manners
15 Ranch Hands + Autumn Trail
16 Hayride + Chocolate Horse
17 High Horse + Hay Fever
18 Horse Tale + Riding Lesson
19 Stage Coach + Horse Trade
20 Purebred + Gift Horse
21 Stable Witch + Saddlebags

22 Photo Finish + Horseshoe
23 Stable Groom + Flying Horse
24 Horse Magic + Mystery Ride
25 Stable Farewell + Yankee Swap
26 Pleasure Horse + Riding Class
27 Horse-Sitters + Gold Medal Rider
28 Gold Medal Horse + Cutting Horse
29 Tight Rein + Wild Horses
30 Phantom Horse + Hobbyhorse
31 Broken Horse + Horse Blues
32 Stable Hearts + Horse Capades
33 Silver Stirrups + Saddle Sore
34 Summer Horse + Summer Rider
35 Endurance Ride + Horse Race
36 Horse Talk + Holiday Horse
37 Horse Guest + Horse Whispers
38 Painted Horse + Horse Care
39 Rocking Horse + Horse Flies
40 English Horse + English Rider
41 Wagon Trail + Quarter Horse
42 Horse Thief + Schooling Horse

Coming soon...

43 Horse Fever + Secret Horse   44 Show Jumper + Sidesaddle

The latest stories from The Saddle Club available now...

New Rider   Hard Hat   Horse Feathers
Trail Ride   Stray Horse   Best Friends

Get the inside story on your favourite character in ...

Lisa: The Inside Story   Carole: The Inside Story   Stevie: The Inside Story